K '83 00066

Mys   Dewhurst, Eileen
         Whoever I am.   Doubleday, 1982
         188 p $11.95

         Crime Club

         I.t

WHOEVER I AM

By Eileen Dewhurst

WHOEVER I AM

EILEEN DEWHURST

PUBLISHED FOR THE CRIME CLUB BY
DOUBLEDAY & COMPANY, INC.
GARDEN CITY, NEW YORK
1983

All of the characters in this book
are fictitious, and any resemblance
to actual persons, living or dead,
is purely coincidental.

Library of Congress Cataloging in Publication Data

Dewhurst, Eileen.
Whoever I am.

I. Title.
PR6054.E95W48 1983   823'.914
ISBN 0-385-18185-X
Library of Congress Catalog Card Number 82–45102

First Edition in the United States of America

Copyright © 1982 by Eileen Dewhurst
All Rights Reserved
Printed in the United States of America

PROLOGUE

At half past two on a Saturday afternoon the nephew collected his uncle from the nursing home to take him for their customary little walk by the sea. They were seen off in the hall by the deputy matron with the usual gush of smiles. The men's smiles faded as they drove through the gates.

"All well?" asked the nephew sharply.

"All well. In fact, I'm feeling better than I've felt for years. Raring to get back to work."

"We can do with you. Samba?"

"Samba seems a bit stronger. Nurses by the moment are commenting on her progress with the establishment 'we.' 'We're better today, aren't we?' 'We've eaten nearly all our breakfast, haven't we?' 'Matron's very pleased with us.'"

"And with you?"

"Oh yes. I think she agrees with my own diagnosis. I expect you to be hearing any moment that I'm fit enough to leave."

"Good. Good." The nephew's hands relaxed on the wheel. "Programme as usual?"

"Including the ice-creams. Of course."

It was still early enough in the year, and cool enough, for there to be plenty of parking space. When they got out of the car the nephew took his uncle by the arm and they began to walk slowly towards the pier head and the small shops.

"All right?"

"Better and better."

The wind whipped their words away and they made no more attempt to talk. Below them on the sands a group of children romped with a furiously barking dog. Two women in plastic bonnets sat motionless and grim-faced on a bench,

braced against the cold sunny day. A young man lounged beside a bicycle. Outside the shops a small crowd stood around.

"Vanilla or strawberry? Large or small?"

"A small strawberry, please. We must leave room for our
tea."

"All right, go and do your deep breathing."

There were a couple of people waiting to be served. When
the nephew came out of the shop, an ice-cream cornet in either hand, his uncle was leaning over the sea rail. When the
nephew nudged an arm against his shoulder he just managed
to turn his head. In his eyes as he collapsed was an expression
of mingled amazement and entreaty. The ice-cream went everywhere.

In the night nurses' cosy lighted booth the kettle was just coming to the boil. One of the two young nurses leaned forward
for the tea caddy and as she straightened up the other nurse
whispered in her ear. Stifling their laughter, both glanced automatically through the glass to the dark silent landing.
Darker and more silent than the bedrooms, where moonlight
through thin curtains gave grey outlines to the furniture and
the humps in the beds, where the breathing of the elderly, the
infirm, and the disturbed rose and fell now on a whistle, now
on a cough, now on a faint moan.

Steam rose within the booth, misting a pyramid on to the
glass. The two capped heads swayed together, and in a bedroom a shadow swayed briefly on a wall. An owl quavered beyond the window, masking the creak of a knee-joint. Then the
creak of a floorboard, the click of a handle, a shadow motionless on a door as a sleeper stirred.

Within the booth, a hand rose to a widely yawning mouth, a
hand stretched out to a biscuit tin. Two heads came together
again, as a choice was made.

A shadow now along the landing wall, no sound on the carpet. Another door-handle turning. One quiet sleeper, the
breathing scarcely to be heard unless one bent close. An arm
outflung as if waiting, a jab and a jerk, the anguished exclama-

tion lost before it reached the door, the unresisting head turned in to the pillow.

The two nurses were sitting back now, a mug cradled in each lap, exchanging friendly, sleepy smiles.

A board creaking, this time on the landing, but the door closing without a sound. The shadow rearing against the wall, finally subsiding. The quavering of a sleeping voice, and of the owls . . .

Eventually one of the nurses got to her feet.

"It's nearly midnight. I'll take a look round."

"No, Jackie, I'll go. Otherwise I'll drop off, which isn't exactly the best thing to do a few minutes before Matron's due back."

"All right, I won't argue. Thanks, Sandra."

The nurse who stayed behind angled the desk lamp on to the small wall mirror and anxiously examined her face. She was still busy on the first pimple when she heard the other nurse scream.

On a fine cold March morning two men went walking in St. James's Park. Each side-stepped the clumps of crocuses as he crossed the grass, raised his eyes occasionally to the hard blue sky, politely threaded the throngs of tourists and bird-watchers on the path beside the lake. They met near the centre of the bridge and leaned side by side on the rail.

"Rumba," murmured the older man, staring down into the grey-blue water. "And then Samba. Not a coincidence."

"Not a coincidence, no."

"I've only read the official report."

The younger man took a paper bag out of his briefcase and began scattering bread on to the water. "The slaughter of the innocents, for God's sake. Felix left Rumba outside while he went into the usual shop to buy the usual ice-cream. When he came out Rumba was leaning over the sea wall dying of heart failure. Felix got him away with as little fuss as possible but the man who helped them to the car did say he'd seen a young man with a bicycle apparently stop and have a word with

Rumba. Of course there was no sign of him. Felix took Rumba to our doctor, and that's where he died. So—death from heart failure, and no record of the skin puncture."

"And Samba . . . smothered in a pillow . . ."

"That's how Samba died, yes. But there was a puncture there, too, which would have brought about almost immediate docility. Could have been tricky but our people got straight on to us and what more natural than that Samba's own doctor should be called in to examine her and issue the death certificate. It's thought to have happened about eleven o'clock. Two young nurses were together in the duty room at the head of the stairs. All the other staff were out of the building between ten and midnight—which of course includes our people. And when Rumba met his end they were all either on duty or otherwise accounted for. There's been rigorous checking out, of course. But—nothing."

"Impossible rigorously to check out the patients."

"Just so. They all have visitors. They all get taken out. In the nature of things, they all regularly go beyond range."

For a few seconds the two men appeared to be watching the convergence of waterfowl beside the bridge.

"Could anyone have got in from outside?"

The younger man folded up his empty paper bag and returned it to his briefcase. "Only if let in. And the two nurses swear they'd done their rounds and all the windows were secured. And even then it would have to have been a window out of range of the duty room—which cuts out downstairs windows, and doors. And what point? Anyone who could unlock a window could use a needle or place a pillow."

"Of course. I think an equation can be discerned. Mole plus patient plus visitor equals successful assassination . . . Any front-runners among the patients?"

"I'm afraid not. Samba had a private room. All the patients had equal access—we were so sure we were a safe house there were no precautions. Rumba shared a room with the three other men, but of course that needn't be of significance in his case. And as I said, all the patients have visitors, get taken out. All were in position, too, when Samba and Rumba were introduced, with the exception of a couple of people who've died—naturally."

"And our mole?"

"One of our people, one surmises. And likely to be on the establishment of the house. Your equation could also embrace safe contact. All those intimate moments in the bathrooms and lavatories between nurse and patient . . . And this time it could have worked the other way—the syringe wasn't found. Our people are being told to stay put, but the patient might have been expected to disappear next time he or she was taken out. No one has gone, and of course a mole on the establishment would be more in need of a safe contact than ever, with all the close scrutiny which has followed the murders."

The older man turned to look at the younger. For the first time their eyes met. "I gather you have a suggestion. Let's walk."

Together the two men strolled off the bridge, crossed the path on to the grass.

"Yes. One of our roving eyes has recently filed details of a subject with the particular qualifications we could do with."

"One of us?"

"No."

"So—rather more expendable than our late lamented."

"That, too." The younger man bent to pick up a chocolate wrapper entwined around some crocuses. He placed it in a litter bin. "I want your permission to recruit. Nothing appears in the subject's past to suggest that the proposition is unwise."

"You may recruit."

"Thank you." The two men halted to look at the sky through a tracery of almond blossom.

"You're thinking of revealing the whole and the true story?"

"Not necessarily. She must be made to mistrust everyone, and she won't do that if she knows she's in a friendly house."

"A woman, is it?" The older man had perhaps made an involuntary movement.

"Yes, a woman." Both men were looking straight ahead, and the brief smile on the younger one's lips went unobserved.

"Well, I leave it to your respected judgement. With the one proviso which I insult your intelligence by mentioning."

"Yes?"

"This time, no one on the establishment is to know."

"Unless and until the enemy in the lounge is discovered. At that point, we must make sure that they do know."

"And reward your recruit by setting her up. I hope she has courage as well as skills."

"That I intend to find out before I commit us. If it goes ahead, I shall be able to present myself at the house with her. I'm not known to anyone."

"Good. No way of introducing anyone on to the staff?"

"I hear there's a lowly post about to become vacant. We can't create an extra job, it would be too obvious, so we'll have to make do with that. At least it will be a good position for keeping an eye on one of our suspects. Not so easy, trying to outwit one's own people. Well, it shouldn't be. But no doubt we'll manage it."

"You will. By the way, I read somewhere recently that white bread isn't especially good for birds."

"I'll bear it in mind."

With the briefest of direct glances, the two men departed as they had arrived.

CHAPTER 1

1

"Mary had a little lamb. Little lamb. Mary had. *Had.*"

The words stuttered out of her, as they always did in moments of stress. And this was acute stress. They had tied her hands behind her back, to the chair, and her ankles to the chair legs. Now they were moving about the room, opening drawers and rummaging. The man said, "What the hell are we worrying about her for? We know she's daft." Perhaps they couldn't help wondering what it might do to her, the violence and the unkindness. Daft people could be sensitive to intention, to a switch from concern to callousness . . . Not that she could understand what was happening, she was nothing beyond one small point of terror and confusion.

"Mary had a little lamb. She had. Mary *had.* A little lamb."

Eventually they stopped searching and came and stood looking down at her. The man had something in his hand and eventually the girl shrugged and they both went out. She went on with the nursery rhymes, more and more feebly, and then the other man, the kind man, came back and untied her. She collapsed in his arms and he laid her on the floor and listened to her heart before backing away in shock and sorrow . . .

She felt, as always, the draught from the curtain as it swept past. She was hidden now, there was no need to go on lying on the floor, but she still felt weak and helpless and she waited, as she did each night, for one of the men to come and help her to her feet. Tonight it was Rupert.

"You were great," he said.

Jonathan took her other hand and as the curtains parted they bowed, with the rest of the cast, to the small, politely clapping audience. The final curtain lasted no more than seconds as the audience had ceased to clap except for two women in the second row, and was moving into the aisles.

It seemed an effort to spring, two at a time, up the steep stone stairs to her dressing-room. Then the two girls arrived.

"You are marvellous," said Christine admiringly, a housemaid from the nineteen-twenties standing behind her and looking in the mirror of the dressing-table where Helen was sitting.

Helen stared at her face, already free of make-up, and wondered vaguely how Christine saw it.

"You really would think you were—well, you know." Blushing, Christine unpinned her lace cap.

"I feel as if I was." Helen untied her own headband, grimacing into the mirror at Christine as she shook her head and sent her smooth cap of grey-white hair swirling in release. "I was always good at the weak-minded. And the old."

She was studying her face, which even now looked too stressful, thin and pointed with fine lines in the dark skin under the eyes.

She was ready to go, as she always was, long before the other two, and when she stepped into the corridor it was deserted.

The night was fine, the sky full of stars. But as she drove away she remembered Christine one night asking her, "Are you going straight home?" And answering "Yes" and saying in her head that she was never going home again. Mrs. Molyneux's wasn't home, and when she got round to finding a flat, as she supposed she would, that couldn't be home, either. Home could only be a certain curve of stair, a certain sound of doors and windows, the shape and colour of a certain room on waking, John . . .

The garage doors had been opened for her, an indication that Mrs. Molyneux was in. She drove between them and negotiated the close ranks of Mrs. Molyneux's gardening impedimenta, got out of the car, and was locking it as the attack came.

The man was only a tall silhouette, the light of the lamp at the gate behind him, and she felt rather than saw the hand fall on her shoulder, curl round the strap of her bag.

It was crazy, it was weak and backsliding, to have as her

only thought that John's photograph was in it, in her wallet, but it seemed to be that thought which made her angry, so that she drew her knee up and kicked out against the silhouette with all her strength, and then dug her teeth into the other hand which came up to try and cut off any screaming. It could have been her own doing—because she had no doubt that the man winced from either her kick or her bite, or both— or it could have been the sudden light from the lamp over Mrs. Molyneux's front door, but as the light came on he turned and ran out of the garage and out at the gate, she heard his feet into the distance as she leaned against the car, indignation giving way to a fear which made her tremble from head to foot. She had got out of the car at night countless times, idly wondering what it would be like to have the tree shadows and the animal and bird sounds turn into a human being with intent to rob or harm her. She had never imagined she would be indignant, she had imagined that right away she would be as shaken as she was now, not able for a few moments to move, and then running straight into the house without fastening up the garage.

"Whatever is it, ducky? I heard the car."

Mrs. Molyneux was standing in the open doorway, infinitely comforting. Helen opened her mouth to explain, then stopped. The man had gone and Mrs. Molyneux had no husband. She heard herself laugh, too loudly.

"It's nothing. I was saying some lines from a play I'm going to read for and I got carried away. I'll shut the door."

There was no one outside, no sound at all on the windless air as she locked up. She stood on the step, listening, until the silence was broken by the distant barking of a dog, then came inside and bolted the door.

Upstairs, gulping a whisky, she decided to call in at the police station in the morning and suggest an evening patrol of the road. Then she took the photo of John out of her wallet and looked at it. She had snapped him in the garden and he was untidy, glancing up from the lawn-mower and smiling. The photo had perhaps just served an unusual purpose, but it was time it went. She tore it slowly into little pieces.

2

From the rocking-chair in which she spent much of the first act of *The Innocent,* Helen had plenty of time and opportunity to observe her audience. But she was so absorbed in her role that she felt as unaware as she pretended to be. When the knock came on the dressing-room door she recognized the rather good-looking well-dressed man who asked to speak to her, although she had not known that she had noticed him among the audience.

He stood silent, observing her, for so long that eventually she must ask him what he wanted.

"I want a word with you in private, Mrs. Markham."

His voice was an attractive murmur.

"Yes?" She felt alarmed, but she had not entirely recovered from the shock of the night before. Christine and Jenny, behind her, were watching in silence, but when she looked at them they resumed the motions of getting ready.

"Not here," said the man gently. "I had thought of the White Swan."

It couldn't be anything to do with John, he had promised to let her know himself if and when he decided to take any legal steps. Even so.

"I don't think . . ."

"Mrs. Markham." The man must have been strikingly handsome a few years earlier, before he had started to put on weight. "Please," he said. "If you prefer it, I can meet you there."

"I do prefer it."

"So you will meet me?" He permitted himself a slight smile. It too was attractive.

"Yes." All at once she felt desperately tired.

"Fifteen minutes?"

"Something like that."

The man inclined his head to her, then to the two girls once more motionless behind her, and went out shutting the door.

"Having him sitting there," said Jenny, "made a difference to the whole performance."

"Was he there all the way through?" Helen sat slowly down at her table.

"Didn't you see? Yes, and paying attention."

"I did see," said Helen absently. And indeed, she saw as if for the first time the concentration of the man's gaze, realized that there had been an intensity about the figure on the end of the third row which was absent from the relaxed man who had called at the dressing-room.

"So you don't know him?" pursued Christine.

"I don't know him."

It had to be something to do with John. So it shouldn't make her nervous. Nothing to do with John should make her nervous now, after the one enormous thing he had done against her.

By the time she reached her car, curiosity was her strongest emotion. And she was aware of being glad not yet to be going back to her silent room.

The lounge at the White Swan had almost emptied, and he was sitting in a low chair close to one of the log fires. He got up as he saw her and indicated the chair opposite. She sank into it.

"Will you have a drink, Mrs. Markham?"

As she felt now she didn't hesitate.

"Whisky, please. Soda."

The waiter was beside them instantly. The stranger looked that sort of man. He ordered two double whiskies.

"I hope it *is* more fulfilling than the amateur stage," he observed, after a silence she was determined not to break.

"At least one doesn't work a play up and then drop it after only three or four performances." She had to force herself not to sound defensive, and was unable to hold back her next remark. "You find it obvious that I've been on the amateur stage?"

The waiter put their drinks on the table. "I do not find it obvious at all. But I know a great deal about you, Mrs. Markham."

It was absurd to feel let down over anything John might do, now. But that he should have had her watched! Even more absurd was the flicker of hope that to have her watched might be to care what she did.

"So you have been engaged by my husband. Why have you come out into the open?"

"Oh, I'm so sorry, Mrs. Markham." The concern was a little too quickly assumed to reflect real feeling. "No, not by your husband. I assure you I have no connection with your husband."

Helen picked up her glass and drank to her disappointment. When she looked up he was still studying her, with clear but objective interest.

She heard the edge on her voice.

"What is it you want, then, Mr. . . . ? I don't think you told me your name."

He had a card in his hand, as abruptly as a conjuror, plain and sparsely printed. Before he withdrew it she read the name Julian Jones and saw S.W.1.

"I came to find you, Mrs. Markham," he said, "because you are such a good actress."

"You're an agent!"

This time her reaction was pure happy surprise, warming her physically. Mr. Jones picked up his glass and slowly drank, not looking at her. When he had set it down he resumed his study of her face, and again she forced herself to stay silent until he spoke.

"Not precisely an agent," he said at last. "At least, not in the sense I think you have in mind. But I have come to offer you a job because of your ability as an actress. Specifically, your ability to become . . . er . . ."

"Mad. I've always been good at that. And being old. Madness and old age. My specialities." She spoke automatically, aware of pleasure ebbing away. He was the representative of some amateurs who had an unusual amount of nerve and initiative.

"So good now, Mrs. Markham, that your fame has spread."

"Really. And the Reddington Repertory Company so obscure."

It wasn't a question, but he must have seen her curiosity in her eyes.

She shivered, not so much from cold as from a sort of anticipation. He called the waiter over and asked for another log on the fire. He asked her if she would like tea.

"Oh yes!"

This time, for the first time, it was an exchange of smiles. He had a dimple in one cheek and in his round chin, and when he turned in half profile she thought she could imagine how he had looked as a boy. Everything about him, including his voice, was soft-edged—cheek, jaw, nose, the white hand which was resting on his knees. His brown hair was smooth, his dark grey suit casually elegant. Not the sort of man who would be spokesman for an amateur dramatic society . . .

"How are you getting on?" he asked her, stretching his legs out to the revived blaze.

"I'm sorry?"

She realized it was the implication of knowledge which had made her nervous, from his first appearance at the dressing-room door.

"Since you left home. It can't be easy, adjusting to a single life, after twelve years of marriage."

Anger rose in her, flooding out the apprehension. She got to her feet, knocking against the arriving tea-tray.

"You or my husband had better write to me, Mr. Jones, rather than play silly games. You can tell him that my hair has already gone white."

"Put the tray down." He spoke first to the hovering waiter. "And you, Mrs. Markham, please sit down again." His hand on her arm, even through the coat she had just shrugged on, was very firm. "I told you the truth when I said I had nothing to do with your husband. Also when I told you I know a great deal about you. Anyone who is to be asked to undertake work of national importance has to be very thoroughly investigated."

"National importance?"

She sat down again and, unresisting, let him take off her coat. He held her shoulders for a second between his hands, in a gesture which she found reassuring, before slipping the coat over the back of her chair and himself sitting down. He poured tea for her. He handed her the cup and saucer and remained leaning slightly towards her so that for the first time she was aware of an agreeable scent.

"Mrs. Markham. You will appreciate the impossibility of maintaining a permanent staff sufficiently versatile to fill all the roles which have to be created to meet the various contingencies which threaten the national interest. So that where particular skills are called for, temporary appointments have to be made. There exists at this moment, in a well-known seaside town, an establishment which is giving cause for concern. On the face of things it's a private nursing home. But there is other activity. Is your tea all right?"

"It's fine." Despite her wariness, it was exhilarating to find herself interested and intrigued. She started as a log in the hearth exploded in a shower of sparks. Mr. Jones smiled.

"I might have been dismayed by so sensitive a reaction, Mrs. Markham, had our little test not revealed that under threat you in fact act first and react later."

She didn't, she couldn't, understand him.

"I admit it for two reasons: to allay anxiety as to the safety of your Mrs. Molyneux. And to show you how important all this is."

Anger and apprehension now swelled together, but could no longer make her want to get up and go.

"You organized that attack on me?"

"That apparent attack, yes. Had you not resisted, your assailant would still have run away. As it was, you inflicted more injury than you sustained."

"I'm glad to hear it."

"Now, as to what we have in mind."

"A guess suggests itself, but it's incredible."

"There is no doubt that the nursing home does accommodate and care for the infirm and the convalescent. But in addition it is a temporary refuge for enemy agents. When they need sanctuary, rest or recuperation. They can sit in the lounge among the genuine clientele with absolute safety. One is doing so at this moment."

"What's the persuasion, Mr. Jones? Russian? Chinese?"

His gaze, which scarcely ever left her, seemed to intensify.

"A fair question, Mrs. Markham. But not, I regret, one that I can answer at this juncture. However, it is not relevant, beyond my assurance that we are up against an enemy. We do not believe that all those who run the nursing home are privy to its second purpose. Some are merely what they seem. As, with the significant exception, are the patients. If only one of them had as sharp eyes and ears, as keen an intelligence, as the adversary! What I am empowered to ask you to do is to become a patient yourself in the nursing home—a woman in the state you have simulated so convincingly for two hours this evening."

"But—everybody else is the other side of the footlights. I couldn't—"

"I think you could. With training. There will be danger, of course. But when we have all done our work, I think the odds will be in your favour."

Mr. Jones smiled at her and drained his glass. "The lady you represented this evening is given to wandering, to picking things up and looking at them. So is the lady who becomes an inmate of Hill House. She will be excellently placed to find out who among her fellow patients is not what he or she seems."

"Do you expect me to accept the job?"

"We think it's likely. You've been used to a role more absorbing than your present one, however much it suits your talents. And your employment is as yet temporary. So that you have no real commitment, no plans or hopes for the future." He went on staring at her, steadily and without compassion. She knew one of the sudden tears had dropped off her lashes and was crawling down her cheek, but he gave no sign of having noticed it. "You have also been used to living rather well. We would pay you a very good salary." He mentioned a sum which for a few seconds took her breath away. "The assignment will come to an end," said Mr. Jones, "and you will be able to do something with the money. Travel, perhaps."

"If I live to enjoy it." She said that, really, because of his smug assumptions about her, to live didn't seem so vital a condition when, as Mr. Jones had expressed it, there were no plans or hopes for the future. It must seem to his superiors that she fulfilled their requirements with extraordinary exactitude.

"On something like this—you can't expect me to give you an answer tonight."

"Of course not, Mrs. Markham. But we should like one as soon as possible. Before our quarry moves on."

"Why don't you just take the place over? Flush everyone out?"

"One can't take fee-paying patients over."

"But you might find evidence as to which patient it is—"

"I should perhaps make it clear from the outset, Mrs. Markham, that you will not be engaged to make any sort of contribution to policy." His face had not changed. "Now, perhaps you will meet me here after the theatre in two nights' time. On Friday?"

They stared at one another, and she thought how little he had really told her.

"Friday, yes," she said. "But I'll come to you. To your office in town. I can manage morning or afternoon."

Some reaction had at last modified his expression, but she didn't know what it was.

"As you wish, Mrs. Markham."

"Forgive me," she said, but not apologetically. "Even doing that I shall be taking a risk. While we've been sitting here I've been thinking about that film where the baddy took over the goody's office at lunch-time and conned Audrey Hepburn into trusting him."

"You're quite right, of course. Can you make it three o'clock on Friday? Too late for a baddy." His face was serious.

"I can. Will you give me your card?"

Mr. Jones didn't hesitate. "There's a man at a desk just inside the building. Ask for Seventh Floor. Julian Jones. And show him the card."

"I'll do that."

Mr. Jones got to his feet, helping her up with the soft white hand which was so unexpectedly firm. They walked out together and he saw her into her car.

"Till Friday, Mrs. Markham."

CHAPTER 2

1

By the morning the thought of accepting Mr. Jones's vacancy seemed as absurd and unlikely as the idea that he had really offered it. But the day after that was her birthday and John did not, of course, acknowledge it. So that by the time she met Mr. Jones for the second time in his office in town Helen was hoping for the reassurance she received.

It came from the building which housed his office, the discreet uniformed man at the desk downstairs, Mr. Jones's name on his door, the response of a secretary and two colleagues to respectively a buzzer and an internal telephone, the atmosphere of ease and familiarity with which Mr. Jones moved about office and corridors, the ubiquitous motifs of OHMS. What more could she ask for? When she had looked and listened, she said yes.

She finished out her week at the theatre. When they offered her a contract she told them, on Mr. Jones's gentle but firm suggestion, that she and her husband had decided to try and make a go of things. She told Mrs. Molyneux this, too. Somehow (as she had to agree with Mr. Jones), it served to cut out any necessity to talk about keeping in touch. And it could be made to appear a consequence of Mr. Jones's appearance in the theatre.

It was a cruel paradox, reflected Helen as she lay in bed in

the mock-tudor house where Mr. Jones had brought her, to
have so many personal memories dredged up in the process of
teaching her to be impersonal.

Perhaps they thought that if the memories were brought to
the surface they would blow away. And of course they wanted
above all else to find out how she reacted. She thought she
reacted far more toughly than she would have done in the days
when she was dependent on John, and happy. They tore at her
personality in the mornings, and even in the recreational afternoons, and after dinner when she and Mr. Jones and the
young woman and one or other of the two young men who bul-
lied her before lunch sat with her watching television or playing Scrabble, she knew the assessment must still be going on.
Yet the young woman, introduced to her as Cora, appeared,
on and off duty, to be two different people. In the mornings
she and the young man of the day devised playlets in which
one of them told Helen something which was not to be di-
vulged and then the other tried to drag it out of her. The traps
were verbal, but they threatened violence. In the afternoons
when it was fine Cora accompanied her into the back garden,
chatting along the gravelled paths and across the lawn as if
she was Helen's friend. She was blonde and beautiful, and said
to be Mr. Jones's daughter.

Other comparable bourgeois residences were visible over
the red brick garden wall, but at first Helen had no idea where
she was, except that she was a two-hour drive from south London: when Mr. Jones picked her up in the car with darkened
windows he began at once to talk, which had prevented her
from concentrating sufficiently to gauge the direction the car
was taking, beyond the first few streets.

The front garden of the house was bounded on the road by
a high holly hedge, and she saw it only from the windows. In-
doors, too, there were restrictions. When she idly tried her
door the first night, she found it locked. When she mentioned
it to Mr. Jones in the morning, he nodded.

"Regulations, Mrs. Markham. You'll understand."

And even if she didn't . . . On his desk there was no sign of the letters Mrs. Gray the housekeeper had just taken in to him. They had slid through the letter-box on to the floor as Helen was crossing the hall, and she had gone towards them with the idea of reading the addresses. But Mrs. Gray had emerged from behind the green baize door to the kitchen, and had reached them first without appearing to hurry.

2

At the end of the first week Mr. Jones told her, gravely but offering no space for commiseration, that he had recently lost his mother. He had therefore had to make arrangements for the care of his sister, who had never been capable of looking after herself.

"So that's how—"

"My sister will be joining us on Monday, Mrs. Markham."

In the second week they made her withstand the mornings in her new persona, react to every conceivable stress short of physical attack as poor Miss Jones senior would react, build up a consistent character. From her ascent to the enormous room at the top of the house, until her descent for lunch, she must be the weak-minded woman who had been backward since childhood, and had as a young girl compounded her weakness by a serious fall on the head. The maintenance of the role through hours, without a script, against bullying odds, was a strain which told on her in tension for the rest of the day, but by the end of the week the character was established down to the smallest detail.

Miss Jones, on her better days, could string a phrase or two together, could make known her needs, which were usually for access to a spot, real or imagined, which had taken her fancy, or to touch and hold. If an object was to hand and portable, Miss Jones would pick it up and handle it—always, to the dictates of some residual mind, without damaging it, and eventually returning it to its place. She didn't require distraction, although she could sometimes appear to be absorbed in a

television programme or a live conversation. She was sensitive
to hostile atmosphere or harsh approach, retreating into furious repetition of her small repertoire of nursery rhymes, which,
in more fragmentary form, were never far from her lips.

Her appearance was unremarkable. She had easy hair, cut
short, and as she liked the idea of putting make-up on her
face, having watched her mother day by day at her dressing-
table, she had a pot of vanishing cream and an old powder
compact. Also a pale lipstick, which she sometimes remembered to smear on, and sometimes didn't. She wore serviceable
dresses which opened sufficiently for her to step into them,
and sensible warm cardigans over them when it was chilly.
At forty-five, she was eight years older than Helen Markham.

"I don't know how you do it, frankly," Cora, relaxed at the
end of the last training session of the week, made Helen think
of Jenny in the dressing-room. "I mean—you're not all that different from yourself, really, and yet you're absolutely different.
And I can't see how. Your hair's lost its chic with that bit of
cutting, and I suppose shoes and dresses . . . You look an entirely different shape, sort of dried up . . . But it's your face,
of course, really. All the life gone. But even your features look—
well—vague. And your mouth's completely different. Did you
teach yourself in the mirror?"

"No. I have to do it from inside. I've had a look at myself
after I've done it, but the action of becoming—Miss Jones—
that happens in my mind, as if I draw the outward evidence of
myself, of what I am, down inside, away from the surface."

"I should have thought there would be a danger of losing
yourself inside as well."

"If I really—get into trouble—it might be the best thing if I
did lose myself inside."

She told Mr. Jones, when he called her into his office, that
she was glad there had been no exercises in this direction.

"It was considered. But it was decided that it might create
a bad feeling between the members of my family which could
prove counter-productive." She was even more chilled that he
should smile.

"But there will be danger."

"At every moment. If you come for one split second out of character. But we are all now confident . . ."

Mr. Jones indicated some unopened post on the desk between them. Helen picked up an envelope. They were outside Bournemouth, in a house called The Laurels.

"The enemy in the lounge. You must try to take him or her unawares—in the night, in the cloakroom at all times when people with minds will not expect to be observed. As Miss Jones you have a unique opportunity. Someone, somewhere, will eventually be a little careless, as it were in front of the cat, or the canary. But he or she will be trained, on a reflex, to spot anything which the cat or the canary could not be doing. He or she will be as vigilant as Helen Markham. And remember too: every member of the staff is your potential enemy."

They stared at one another in silence. She broke it to ask softly, "Am I going—soon?"

"You're going tomorrow. We think you're ready. And you have to be ready, in case our quarry moves on."

"It's been the longest two weeks of my life."

CHAPTER 3

1

There are still to be found on the East Cliff at Bournemouth a number of Victorian gothic houses in beige brick, although they are being steadily eroded by blocks of flats. Most of them are now private hotels, but a few are nursing homes accommodating a dozen or so of the elderly and infirm.

Hill House was among these, its name chiselled into the heavy sandstone of its gateposts. It had three storeys and two raised gothic eyebrows, and would have been imposing in its curved pine-planted road before the eight-storey flats went up next door. It had once been a hotel, and it was for the hotel that the lounge had been extended in glass, so that from the road half the inmates could be seen sitting in the window. Between the window and the low wall, however, a large square of lawn surrounded by bushes and flowers allowed some privacy and made up for the lack of garden at the back.

Helen had taken her departure from The Laurels as her entrance on stage, and sat slumped in her seat throughout the drive, responding in trailing phrases to Mr. Jones's cheerful banal remarks (he also appearing to consider the play had begun), or not responding at all. Only as he stopped the car on the forecourt of Hill House she murmured:

"These are my last words."

He answered as softly, "Good luck to you." His hand gripped her shoulder. "Now, sweetheart," he said bracingly. Even when her door was open Helen made no move, and Mr. Jones half lifted her out on to the gravel. The car door shut noisily in the quiet air. Mr. Jones picked up the suitcase, took her arm.

He rang the bell, they stood side by side waiting for the blue and white shape to loom beyond the frosted panels. When it appeared, when the lock rattled and they began the ascent of the shallow steps, Helen stumbled involuntarily in the apprehension of her first encounter.

It was the deputy matron, plump and fair. She smiled approvingly at Mr. Jones, indulgently at the vague lady by his side.

"Miss Jones, then?" she inquired, her glance quickly back on the man.

"Yes, here we are."

Miss Jones was murmuring to herself as her brother guided her into the chintzy warmth of the hall. The deputy matron took the suitcase out of his hand, called a hurrying nurse to take it upstairs.

"This way to the lounge, Mr. Jones."

Helen, staring at the deputy matron, realized that lady was

agreeably impressed by Miss Jones's brother. Also realized, beneath her tension, the advantage of being able to stare uninhibitedly at whom she would.

"There's a nice chair waiting for your sister." The three of them were moving slowly across the hall. "And I gather you'll be having her to stay in your home at weekends. How very kind . . . dear Miss Jones," added the deputy matron, still looking at Mr. Jones.

Helen's sensations were not unfamiliar, they were the sensations she experienced every time she was on stage in a major role. It was the intensity of them, this time, which was new. Always she had felt that her life depended on her performance. Now she knew that it did.

There seemed, of course, to be little audience reaction in the lounge at Hill House. The deputy matron piloted Helen to an empty chair across from the window and placed a stacking chair for Mr. Jones to sit near her.

"I'll see you before you go, Mr. Jones." Helen, looking straight ahead, heard the heavy steps cross the room. A rather silly woman, perhaps. But *every member of the staff is your potential enemy* . . .

"Hello, dear." The white-haired lady in the next chair patted Helen's hand. In the middle of the room one pair of eyes snapped open, stared a long moment, snapped shut . . .

"You know, I think it's quite a nice day."

The white-haired old gentleman got to his feet, walked a few steps vaguely towards them, and hovered. Helen was aware of those ladies who were still in charge of their minds and their movements shifting slightly in their seats. There is a feeling of uneasiness engendered by anyone who stands expectantly by.

"Experience has taught us," murmured a thin, sharp-faced woman to Mr. Jones, "that Mr. Thomas will move on or back only if ignored over a period of minutes. His anecdotes and observations, with their invariable emphases and pauses, recur as exactly as gramophone records. It could be three or four times in one afternoon."

"I was saying, Miss Duncan, I think it's really quite a nice day."

The sharp-faced woman sniffed. The kindly gaze moved on to Helen's neighbour.

"Mrs. Anthony . . ."

"Nice and bright." The words came reluctantly from Mrs. Anthony's pale young visitor. "But there's a nasty wind."

"Is that so?" Mr. Thomas's kindly face expressed riveted interest. "I thought it looked quite a nice day." The eyes moved on again, reached Mr. Jones. "Ah!" Mr. Thomas's smile widened. He rocked on his feet in anticipation. Mr. Jones was looking at his knees. "If you'll excuse my mentioning it." Mr. Thomas addressed Mr. Jones very politely. "Isn't it you who goes up to Liverpool on business? I used to go up to Liverpool. Do you by any chance know—"

"I'm afraid you've got the wrong chap." Mr. Jones offered a quick rueful smile.

"*Sh!*" The admonishment came from the chair directly in front of the television set.

"Mrs. Wayne-Jenkins," murmured Miss Duncan. "A tartar of formidable proportions. In every sense."

"I think they want us to keep quiet," said Mrs. Anthony's visitor to Mr. Thomas.

"What's that?" With unwavering smile Mr. Thomas leaned towards her. "I didn't quite catch—"

"I think they want us to—"

"Be *quiet*, Mr. Thomas!" scolded Mrs. Wayne-Jenkins.

Mr. Thomas straightened up, still smiling. The young woman beside Mrs. Wayne-Jenkins said feebly, "We could always go upstairs, Auntie, and watch your set . . ." and was quelled by a glance.

"Your cough's gone, then, Mother?"

It was the pale young woman addressing Helen's neighbour. Miss Anthony, it must be, there was no ring on her finger.

"Quite gone, thank you, dear."

"Enjoyed your lunch today?"

"The food's very nice, thank you, dear!"

"It's appalling!"

The voice came from the row of chairs facing the television. Mrs. Wayne-Jenkins, exaggeratedly absorbed in the programme, had obviously not spoken. The woman beyond her was as obviously asleep. Miss Jones's steady gaze was on the twisted lips of the grey-faced lady who had noticed her arrival, who sat so uncomfortably motionless in the nearest chair, and Helen saw them move.

"The food's disgusting." The eyes remained closed.

"Oh, surely not." Miss Anthony gave a worried glance at her mother.

"Oh, surely!" The lips were more noticeably curled. The eyes opened briefly, stared into Miss Anthony's, snapped shut. "But I'm ill, I can't . . ." There was the suspicion of a shrug, a hand like a bird's claw rose, dropped back on the arm of the chair.

"Mrs. Wellington," murmured Miss Duncan.

"Yes, Mrs. Wellington." Again, only the lips moved. Helen thought she had never seen anyone sit still with such strain.

"She has very acute hearing," breathed Mr. Jones.

Mr. Thomas shuffled back to his seat and sat heavily down, his smile faded to a look of benevolence. Miss Anthony leaned across to the sharp-faced woman whom Helen was still not quite able to place as inmate or visitor.

"Is my mother really all right, do you think, Miss Duncan? It's so difficult to be sure. She's the sort of person who never complains. Everything for the best in the best of all possible worlds."

"Which this isn't, of course," said Miss Duncan briskly. "But, it's not so bad, as such places go. The staff are kind and the food's good enough. Don't worry about your mother."

"I wish she was in a room with you. But I imagine you've got your own room."

"I haven't got my own room, no." Miss Duncan picked something off her skirt.

"Oh, I should have thought—"

"Thank you, yes, I'm not senile yet." Miss Duncan looked round with an air of defiance, bringing Mr. and Miss Jones back into her orbit. "But I don't have very much money. 'Distressed gentlewoman' is, I believe, the phrase which is still used, although now perhaps with a certain comic emphasis."

"Yes. I mean, no. I'm sorry . . ."

"Don't be. Excuse me."

Miss Duncan would no doubt have wished to flounce out of the room, and Helen was sorry to see her have to struggle to her feet. When she was upright she walked slowly, with very short steps, to the door and out.

"Miss Duncan has a toothache," said Mrs. Anthony, patting her daughter's hand.

"Has she?"

"I think so . . ." The thread of memory appeared to break off, Mrs. Anthony gazed round perplexed. She was a nice-looking old lady with a fresh complexion and pretty white hair. "I think they said they were taking her to the dentist."

"I've got a toothache," said Mrs. Wellington, still without opening her eyes. "I've told them, but nobody does anything about it."

A young nursing sister looked up from her unrewarding blandishment of a wild-eyed lady in the window.

"Your daughter's made an appointment for you for next week, Mrs. Wellington," she said with cheerful reproach. "She's going to take you herself."

"Miss Duncan's tooth started to ache after she had some bacon," said Mrs. Wellington, blinking for a sharp second at Helen. "I think she broke it. She's lucky to have any teeth to break at her age. I've only got ten, but they ache enough for twenty."

A door was opened across the room, allowing a glimpse of tables. A nurse was seen and then heard, clattering crockery. The young woman sitting beside Mrs. Wayne-Jenkins half got to her feet as if on a reflex, glanced at the clock on the mantelpiece, gave a sickly smile, and sat down again.

"Yes, you needn't go yet, Veronica," said Mrs. Wayne-Jenkins tartly. "They always start the tea at least fifteen minutes before they serve it. Unless, of course, you are anxious to leave."

"Of course not, Auntie."

"Anyone would be anxious to leave here," observed Mrs. Wellington.

"I wish she wouldn't talk like that," murmured Miss Anthony.

"It won't affect your mother, I'm sure," soothed Mr. Jones. It was unnerving, his dual capacity to soothe and to alarm. "It won't affect anyone." Mrs. Wellington opened her eyes and fixed them on Mr. Jones. "Whatever I say, no one listens."

"They get tired of your complaining." This from Mrs. Wayne-Jenkins.

Mrs. Wellington closed her eyes. The nursing sister left the wide-eyed lady in the window and came to perch on the arm of Miss Duncan's empty chair.

"You must be Mr. and Miss Jones. So sorry I wasn't . . . But sometimes Miss Welch . . . I'm Sister Wendy, I'll be helping to look after your sister." She was a pretty girl, with wide-apart blue eyes and fair wavy hair springing free of her cap. Mr. Jones responded. Mrs. Anthony put her hand out and the nurse took it. "It's nearly tea-time, isn't it?" Mrs. Anthony asked.

"You're quite right," said Sister Wendy, "but not just yet."

"Mr. Weston . . ." Mr. Thomas looked towards the door. A small thin man with sparse sandy hair, very red cheeks and a sharp nose was ambling across the room, his eyes fixed on some far horizon. "Is it tea-time?" he asked in a husky voice, clearing his throat both before and after speaking.

"For heaven's sake!" said Mrs. Wayne-Jenkins.

Sister Wendy bent towards Mr. Jones.

"Mrs. Wayne-Jenkins has her own room," she said confidentially, "but of course her bed's in it, and one doesn't entertain in one's bedroom. The old school. So when she has a visitor we have the pleasure of her company in the lounge. She has her meals upstairs. But these ladies will be your sister's table companions."

"I'm sure she'll be happy. I'll leave her with you now. Goodbye, sweetheart." Mr. Jones bent over and lightly kissed the corner of Helen's mouth. She was aware of panic. The very ease of her entrance, the passivity of her role, were hazards.

They could cause her to relax her guard, to resume for moments which might be fatal her own life in her head. Through the long spaces of doing nothing, she must not think of irrelevant things. Not be lulled to a false sense of security. As if to underline the warning, the television, clearly visible from Miss Jones's chair, was showing a repeat of a programme she had enjoyed.

"Julian . . . I don't . . ."

"I'll see you tomorrow. You'll be coming home with me then, for the weekend. But I really think you'll have more fun here. Goodbye, sweetheart."

She heard his feet on the polished floor, but didn't turn her head. Mrs. Wellington was looking at her again. She closed her eyes quickly when they caught Helen's. But Miss Jones couldn't catch anybody's eye, that was the point.

No reaction.

Mrs. Wellington really did look, between glances, as if she was asleep. It was tempting to think of her right away as the enemy in the lounge. She might seem rather too obviously a candidate, but her credentials would have been as impeccably prepared as Helen's own. And if not Mrs. Wellington then the masterful Mrs. Wayne-Jenkins with her private room, or the sharp-minded Miss Duncan, whose faltering steps could be assumed . . .

She had not been hired to speculate, but to gather and present facts.

Helen saw her hand trembling on the arm of her chair. She closed her eyes for a moment, a relief which her role allowed her, bracing and encouraging herself, and when she opened them it was the cosy and amiable Mrs. Stoddart who was staring at her, even leaning forward and holding out a hand. Suppressing her instinct to respond, Helen stared back.

"You'd like a cup of tea, dearie?" The voice was genteel Edinburgh.

"Tea . . . I don't . . ." faltered Miss Jones.

"I must go, Mother." Miss Anthony got to her feet. Helen was aware of their embrace.

"You're lucky, you know, Mrs. Anthony," said Sister Wendy,

"to have such a good daughter. And I think Miss Jones is lucky too, to have a good brother." For an unnerving moment the blue eyes smiled into Helen's. *No reaction.* Miss Anthony set off for the door, and Helen felt the cold sweat on her back.

"We're all going to have a nice cup of tea. Come along!" Sister Wendy swung off across the room without, Helen was certain, looking at Miss Jones again. But she felt weak from the encounter, breathless. There was no doubt she had learned, within half an hour of its beginning, that she had underestimated the strain of her assignment.

2

The transition from lounge to dining-room was as painless as could be devised: the rooms opened into one another and there were no steps.

Several of the inhabitants had already made their way through, perhaps from a desire to be on with the next distraction in a world where these were few and far between, perhaps because they could not relinquish a suspicion that someone might, despite precedent, usurp their time-honoured positions. This must surely be so with the permanently distraught Miss Welch, whom Helen had seen get up as soon as Sister Wendy left her alone at the window, and rush at the dining-room door. The three gentlemen also had taken themselves through slightly in advance of the announcement: Mr. Thomas, Mr. Weston who reminded Helen of a robin, and Mr. Corlett, a small white-haired American. Mrs. Anthony appeared to be afraid of being left behind, and called gently to the nurses. Mrs. Wellington was so placed in the lounge that she was able to put out her bird claw as a nurse went by and pluck at the sleeve, so that she was one of the first to be escorted into the dining-room. Not that she really needed support in walking, once she was on her feet, any more than Mrs. Anthony did. Helen's other neighbour Mrs. Charlesworth, tall and strong, had sat motionless and silent since Miss Jones's arrival, and had to be guided as if blind. Mrs. Stoddart, once set in motion, tended to advance in the correct direction. Miss

Jones, this first time, sat on in her lounge chair, reciting *Mary had a little lamb* with the intensity she tended to manifest in moments of particular disorientation.

So Helen was the last person to be slotted into her place at one of the three small tables which gave to Hill House a fleeting air of still being the private hotel it once was.

She stared round expressionlessly at her neighbours, and beyond them. Now she was at right angles to Mrs. Anthony she could see how pretty the old lady had been. Miss Duncan was on Miss Jones's other side, nearer than in the lounge, meagre and bosomless in beige and brown, brown hair permed to the texture of wool, skin like light brown paper, intelligence and understanding, bitter-tinged, in the darting brown eyes and small thin features. Opposite to Miss Jones was Miss Protheroe. Helen had noticed Miss Protheroe in the lounge, mute and motionless beside the window, staring out or else down at her lap. But now, at the table, she was amazed at the normality of Miss Protheroe's response. Miss Jones stared at the thin small creature with the wispy bun, Helen listened to her and Miss Duncan. While welcoming the revelation that these two ladies were capable of holding an intelligent conversation, she recognized another potential hazard: she could become absorbed in it . . .

The courteous Mr. Corlett leaned across from one of the other tables. "Ladies!" He raised a tea-cup towards them.

"I haven't got anything in my cup!" said Mrs. Wellington peevishly.

"It's all right, dear, I'm on my way." The dark nurse was going round with the teapot. When everyone was served she encouraged Helen's cup between her hands and Helen raised it and drank, regretting the abundance of milk. Mr. Jones would have to mention it . . . Oh God, and the sugar . . . The nurse now was taking the top off her boiled egg. Helen shuddered.

"All right, dear?" asked the nurse absently.

"All right . . . I want to . . . Let me . . ."

It had been an involuntary shudder, a sudden raw realization that she was sitting within feet and inches of people who, if they knew the normality of her mind, would kill her. Eventually.

"Spoon, please." Helen steeled herself to turn her blank face up towards the nurse.

"Very well, dear." The nurse looked at her without seeing her, the sort of look Mr. Jones said they had banked on when they were first deciding what to do.

"Thank you." Miss Jones had, after all, been well brought up. "Hickory, dickory, dock!" She tackled the egg.

Helen was surprised and almost amused to find herself hungry. Fortunately, Mr. Jones had told them his sister was accustomed to finish what was put in front of her. Which reminded her that it was her own fault about the sugar. And about the snail's pace of eating, which she had decided on in order to get as far away as possible from the habits of Helen Markham. John had always teased her about the speed with which she put paid to her meals . . . While she slowly chewed small mouthfuls, Helen let her glance drift round the room.

No Mrs. Wayne-Jenkins, who ate upstairs. There were two other ladies who ate upstairs, who stayed upstairs all the time, because they were apparently too unwell to come down. Cora had suggested them as an early object of her nocturnal wanderings . . .

Mr. Thomas was seated with Mrs. Wellington, Mrs. Charlesworth, and Mrs. Barker. Mrs. Barker, the woman with whom Miss Jones would be sharing a bedroom. Appearing to be incapable of walking without a Zimmer frame, and certainly showing evidence of physical deterioration in the ravaged face still full of intelligence, the twisted body. Helen liked the expression of Mrs. Barker's face, the way she smiled, the clear gaze. Surely such things must indicate innocence . . . *Your job to observe, ours to deduce,* Mr. Jones had said, not smiling.

Mrs. Wellington was looking at her again. Foiling her instincts was probably the hardest part of her role. She had to stop herself turning abruptly away, to keep her eyes drifting slowly past Mrs. Wellington. At least her assumed blankness simplified the basic task of observation.

"How nice it is to have Miss Jones with us," said Miss Protheroe to the table.

At the third table Mr. Corlett was talking steadily and mellifluously to Mr. Weston, while Mrs. Stoddart smiled vague approval and Miss Welch turned her large frightened eyes from one to the other. It was hard not to think there must be something specific which was terrifying Miss Welch, but there couldn't be. She always looked the same, a middle-aged gypsy with wild hair and eyes, forever at a pitch of apprehension . . .

"Are you all right, dear?"

Miss Protheroe was speaking to Miss Jones. The pale blue eyes were as shrewd as they were kind. Helen stared into them, her scalp prickling.

"Thank you very much . . ." she faltered.

"That's right." Miss Protheroe turned to Mrs. Anthony. Helen wiped the palms of her hands down her bib.

3

Being the last to be helped out of the dining-room would afford a good opportunity of watching everyone as they drifted or were escorted away. But the chance would regularly recur, and it was time Miss Jones exhibited her announced prevailing characteristic. Helen got up while everyone was still at table, and wavered towards the door which led from the dining-room into the hall.

"Miss Jones!" The dark-haired nurse fell into step beside her. "Don't you want to go and sit down in the lounge?"

"Want . . . going out . . ." mumbled Helen, continuing unsteadily but firmly on her way. "Going . . ."

"All right." The nurse smiled at her, sped back to catch Mrs. Stoddart who was falling out of her chair. Helen crossed the hall as unpurposefully as she could manage and went into the cloakroom, full of thanks for Miss Jones's independence. When she came out of the cloakroom she drifted on to where the hall narrowed, passed the unmanned staff desk, pushed open the kitchen door.

The large front kitchen was deserted, and there was the

sound of voices punctuated by the clash of crockery from the inner kitchen beyond.

She wanted to brace herself for her first unwarranted entry at Hill House but she couldn't, she was on stage all the time in this theatre in the round, there might be someone at her back and she must continue to drift forward, push the inner door wide, go on walking, up to the big centre table, pick up the glass (as Miss Jones picked up so many things in her casual path) and examine it . . .

"And what's all this?"

Helen looked up, slowly, into the face of the large blonde woman who had just spoken loudly and kindly, as if to a deaf child. Had there been a second of wariness in the eyes? Another woman, a girl really, darted forward and took the glass out of her hand, setting it back on the scrubbed table. Helen offered no resistance, standing there staring while the blonde woman said, on a laugh, "Well, now, who are you?"

As she wavered round the table, Helen was aware of the girl shrugging her shoulders and dragging her feet as she walked slowly over to the sink.

"I want to go . . . Can you tell me where I can find . . ." She put her hands out, as if measuring the space between the fat lady and the table.

"I don't think you *can* go today, lovey," said the fat lady cheerfully, "they're not open."

"Not open." Helen turned slowly away. Sometimes Miss Jones returned to a more orthodox place, sometimes she stayed where her wanderings had taken her. Helen sat down in the old armchair by the door. It was comfortable, and made her aware that she was tired. So Miss Jones must not have a nap. She stared across the room. The girl was washing up and the blonde woman was tidying things away.

"Some right nutters here," said the girl, not turning round.

"I don't like to hear you talking like that, Tracy."

"She can't understand me."

"That's not the point, my girl. And some of them can understand, you'd be surprised."

"Sorry, Mrs. Roberts, sorry."

"Can't have the ladies and gentlemen being offended," pursued Mrs. Roberts. Her white overall had short sleeves and her stout elbows were red. Helen had a confirmed impression of energy and competence. Also of humour.

"How long do we have the pleasure of this one, then?" Tracy half-turned from the sink, dotting the tiled ochre floor around her with blobs of soapy water.

"I don't know this one's habits," said Mrs. Roberts. Helen continued to stare vacantly ahead of her. "She's a rum one, I suppose," said Mrs. Roberts, turning away and opening a cupboard. "But harmless. I'm sure."

Decisive footsteps sounded across the tiled outer kitchen.

"Good afternoon, Matron." Mrs. Roberts again stopped what she was doing. "Tracy!"

"Good afternoon, Matron."

Helen stared at the matron, able to look her fill at the tall, slim, still young and attractive woman with the authoritative manner. The mouth was tight and the gleam in the eyes could be an enjoyment of power for power's sake. The impression of competence, of a discipline which avoided the least wasteful gesture, was very strong.

"Mrs. Roberts." Matron looked from her to Tracy. Mrs. Roberts made a ruefully humorous gesture towards the armchair.

"So I see." Matron pursed her lips.

"She's all right," said Mrs. Roberts heartily.

But how easy it was going to be, whatever she saw, whatever she heard, to think it was significant.

"Of course," said Matron coldly. She had not looked directly at Miss Jones. She moved to the table. "I'd like to talk about menus, Mrs. Roberts. Can you come to my office when you're ready?"

"I'll come now, Matron. Tracy'll finish off."

"How are you settling in, Tracy?" snapped Matron.

The girl glanced at Mrs. Roberts, mumbled something.

"She's all right," said Mrs. Roberts, but less indulgently than she had spoken of Miss Jones.

"Tracy?" posed Matron. It was definitely a snub for Mrs. Roberts.

"All right, I suppose. Thank you."

"Don't thank me. Thank Mrs. Roberts." Matron gave the large lady a wintry smile, walked quickly across the kitchen and turned at the door. "When you're ready, Mrs. Roberts."

"I'll be right up."

Helen waited with interest for the reaction to Matron's visit, but from Mrs. Roberts there was none, not even in the expression of her face. Tracy made a face privately, into the sink. Mrs. Roberts took off her overall and hung it on an inner door.

"Shouldn't like to get the wrong side of *her*," ventured Tracy at last, leaning an elbow on the dresser.

"That's enough, young lady!" Mrs. Roberts moved quickly, and had flipped the girl's arm to her side, making her stumble. "You just finish tidying up in here," she said, not unkindly, "and then you can go off."

"Yes, Mrs. Roberts," said Tracy listlessly, after Mrs. Roberts's retreating back. Helen waited a few moments, until she was certain there was going to be nothing more to see beyond Tracy's perfunctory movements about the kitchen, then wavered to her feet and started to move slowly towards the door. It was a shock first, then a pleasant surprise, that Tracy should be so quickly at her side, saying,

"Come on, then, are you all right?"

"Nice girl . . . All right, yes."

She was accompanied, a warm hand through her arm, back to the hall, and when Tracy left her she stood there for a moment, wondering what to do next. One advantage of her role was that the more time she stood or sat in thought the more she consolidated her character. This time, the decision was taken for her.

"Going to sit down, then, Miss Jones?"

It was Sister Wendy.

"Sit down . . . Yes . . ."

"I'm going off duty," said Sister Wendy, as she deposited Helen in her chair. "See you all tomorrow!"

Helen was surprised at the number of hands lifted in vague salute, even Mrs. Wellington's.

The lounge was almost exactly as it had been on her arrival.

At least she appeared to have established how little Miss Jones was going to worry the staff of Hill House.

Two hours up and one to go before a nurse would come and suggest she might like to go to bed.

On television there was the final part of a serial Helen had been following. Having made a sortie, and anticipating little in the way of relaxation during the night, she allowed herself to watch it.

CHAPTER 4

1

Managed to be in bed when Mrs. Barker was brought up to room, nurse paid me no real attention. Mrs. B. supervised and helped through all bedtime ritual. Appears genuinely incapacitated. Speaks to Miss Jones now and then as if to pet dog. Don't think she sleeps well, although had not got out of bed by 1:30 A.M. when I left the room. Moaned and tossed as I went past, but didn't appear to be aware. Isn't deaf so could have been asleep.

Names of patients on outsides of doors, helpful. Mrs. Wayne-Jenkins and Mrs. Wellington have own rooms, also two women who don't come downstairs. Didn't go into these, but into room where three men sleep, double room which Miss Welch shares with empty bed, two-bedded room shared by Miss Duncan and Mrs. Stoddart, and room with Mesdames Protheroe, Charlesworth and Anthony. Moved about freely, picked up this and that, no reactions beyond continuation of nose and throat noises, whimpers, groans, etc. which sound real enough.

Then back to landing and stood staring through glass door

marked Night Staff. *Nurse Sandra dozing, jumped as I turned handle, but already encountered and recognized Miss Jones. Friendly. I sat in other chair and she said, "You won't tell any tales, will you?" and dozed off again. No sense of vigilance, papers strewn about desk. After a few moments got up and looked at papers—patients' requirements and what to do if any individual taken ill. Nurse opened eyes while I was standing handling paper-knife. Suggested sleepily that I went back to bed which I did, unaccompanied. Obvious consensus that Miss Jones can manage herself, and is harmless.*

Dressed by 8:30 when breakfast brought in. Ate in armchair on portable table, Mrs. Barker in bed. Sat there while Mrs. B. was dressed, observing handicaps. Then to Mrs. Wayne-Jenkins. Mrs. W-J cutting toenails, foot up on chair, wearing (old-fashioned satin) underwear, hair in net. Annoyed but not alarmed. Said, "I don't pay for this!" and rang bell. Wandered round room till nurse came: obviously own furniture, good, bureau with empty lock, no papers visible. Books in small bookcase and on table middle-brow classic paperbacks, Howard Spring, Taylor Caldwell, etc. Let myself be guided on to landing by nurse, who seemed more sympathetic to Miss Jones than to Mrs. W-J.

Then to men's room again, where door open. Mr. Corlett alone in armchair. (Mr. Thomas later found in lounge, Mr. Weston in neither lounge nor bedroom.) Mr. Corlett made great show of welcome, got up, indicated chair which Miss Jones ignored. Wandered about and he resumed seat, returned to newspaper, but half watching, I felt with instinct more of hospitality than suspicion. Mr. C. had American paperback novel on locker. Mr. Thomas nothing. Mr. Weston some British paperbacks, thrillers and adventures. Went out when I'd been round the room, and downstairs.

No incidents in lounge, beyond Mrs. Charlesworth coming to life for furious ten minutes. I gather violent only with tongue, and if restrained, but Mrs. Anthony and Mrs. Stoddart seemed frightened and Miss Protheroe immediately rang bell. Mrs. C. told Mrs. Barker she had a hole in her stocking as if personal affront. Told Mrs. Wellington not to stare, told Mr.

Thomas, when he tried to be smiling gallant, that he was a silly, a silly man, over and over to a shriek. Miss Welch couldn't look more scared than normal expression, so no reaction, nor from Mrs. Wellington who kept her eyes shut, Miss Protheroe who was back at window, staring out. Mrs. Barker looked sad, Miss Duncan said twice, "What a performance!" Mrs. C. rocking about on her feet, pushed nurse and nearly knocked her over when she tried to restrain her. Then suddenly sat down and was transfixed again. Struck me as much easier role to play than Miss Jones.

OBSERVATIONS ON PATIENTS

GENERAL: *Have been close enough to each patient to be convinced, from my experience in the theatre, that none of them is in any kind of disguise which relies on make-up.*

MRS. ANTHONY: *Nice mild old lady, very attached to daughter. Frightened of Mrs. Charlesworth's rage and generally inclined to be anxious. Not a hundred per cent in touch.*

MRS. BARKER: *See above. Has a newspaper delivered and reads books. Heard nurse telling her her son was coming today but had left before he arrived.*

MRS. CHARLESWORTH: *If not in catatonic trance, then in furious rage. Responds at table to spoon or cup actually touching mouth. I suspect intermittent incontinence.*

Helen put her pen down, wrinkling her nose at the unwelcome memory. She tried to outstare the net curtain on her window which it was forbidden to lift aside, but could see only the red smudge of the garden wall, lightening at its foot where there was blossom, a brown of house beyond the wall, a grey which did duty for lawn and sky.

MR. CORLETT: *Heard Sister Wendy explaining he'd had a stroke while visiting his married daughter in this country, and so stayed on. Almost cloyingly courteous. Able to walk unaided and seems clear in mind.*

MISS DUNCAN: *Very intelligent, appears to have difficulty walking. Reads, with apparent absorption. Cynical stance.*

MISS PROTHEROE: *Very observant, without appearing to be. Hardly takes gaze off window, but waves when anyone calls a general goodbye. Talks intelligently at table with Miss Duncan, to whom she has opposite stance, i.e., always seeing the best where Miss D. sees the worst. She and Mrs. Roberts in kitchen have given me my shrewdest looks yet. Frail, and benefits from a helping arm, but doesn't need one.*

MRS. STODDART: *In her own cosy world, it appears, dominated by idea of having tea. Apparently timid (scared of Mrs. Charlesworth's rage).*

MR. THOMAS: *North Country courtesy. Apparently slow-thinking. Slow-speaking, repetitive. Generally thought a bore.*

MRS. WAYNE-JENKINS: *Miss Duncan's description can't be bettered: "a tartar of formidable proportions." Gave short shrift to Miss Jones when I invaded, but that was understandable.*

MISS WELCH: *Looks terrified at all times. Always turns towards any action or speech. Speaks herself only when she wants something or is pressed for a response. Voice as distraught as appearance.*

MRS. WELLINGTON: *Appears to sleep most of the day, looks ill, she and Miss Protheroe say she is ill. Certainly frail on her feet, but can walk unaided. Very keen ears and often joins in quiet conversations of other people, which makes me suspect appearance of sleep. Obviously intelligent. So full of complaint if she was acting one would say the part was overwritten.*

If she was acting . . . Helen gave a dreadful involuntary shudder, then, as exaggeratedly, giggled.

MR. WESTON: *Chirpy little man, appears fit if frail. As mentioned above, wasn't to be seen during the morning.*

Apparently. He or she appears. She was already frustrated by the repetition of the word and the phrase. But it was another word with which Mr. Jones took issue.

"Nothing is obvious, Mrs. Markham," he said gently, when he had called her into the office three hours after their return from Hill House and one hour after his receipt of her report. Anxious, she had written it at once, before changing her drab "Miss Jones" clothes. "Are you, for instance, obvious? We hope not.

"However—" Mr. Jones tapped the sheets of paper on the

desk before him, smiled at her—"this *is* the sort of thing we want, Mrs. Markham. And I think also you had better set down—any instinctive reactions. This would not be the same thing as recording deductions. You see the difference?"

"It means, then, that you don't want me to suppress instinctive feelings, as taking up good observation time?"

"It means that, yes."

His eyes held that intensified look. Helen knew that she sometimes slightly disconcerted him, but it was impossible to tell whether this was because she was sharper than he expected, or bolder, less intimidated by the unwritten laws of his profession than were his other subordinates. Or less aware of them. Surely they had had a more orthodox grounding?

"Sit down, Mrs. Markham," said Mr. Jones, not looking up from the report, "and have a glass of sherry."

"Thank you."

He handed her a glass, raised the other. "Your health, Mrs. Markham."

"Ah yes, my health." They had one of their rare smiling exchanges. Mr. Jones sat down in the other armchair, on the near side of his desk. He looked at her with the interest he never attempted to disguise.

"How are you? You left the stage—" he consulted his watch— "just over three hours ago, and have been working since. Are you all right?"

"I'm fine." She laughed at her surprise. He noticed it.

"You wouldn't have expected to be?"

"Well . . . I don't suppose anybody would *expect* to be, doing something like this for the first time. But apart from that . . ."

"Yes?"

"I've always thought of myself as—well, as rather soft. The last one to have an iron nerve. Part of my image of myself, I suppose, when I was—with my husband. He seemed to be the strong one."

"Hence your surprise."

"Yes. Not quite for the first time." She remembered her fury at the assailant who had tried to take her bag off her shoulder.

"No, of course not." He went on looking at her.

"I must admit, though," she said, "I found the first encounters at Hill House, the first being looked in the eye and not reacting—"

"Alarming. Of course."

"And having to resist instincts of self-preservation. Like restraining myself from turning my head away."

"Naturally." He leaned slightly towards her. "Confess it also, though. There were parts of your performance you enjoyed."

She went to deny it, then paused. "I don't know if enjoy is the word. Perhaps it is. There *was* a sort of pleasure in being able to stare people in the face, go where I liked, handle what I liked. Rather like being invisible."

"I should think that describes the sensation very well." Watching his thoughtful face reminded her suddenly of the Reddington Rep, and the dressing-room that first night. She went on with a pang of regret for something, she didn't know what.

"It's extraordinary. Here I'm stimulated, stretched out to be as bright as I can be—even at meals, and after dinner, there's never a time at The Laurels when I feel it's wise to be dim. And at Hill House no stimulus at all, the clock round."

"The perpetual stimulus of danger." Mr. Jones got to his feet, put his empty glass down on the desk. "You've made a good start."

"Thank you." She got up too, taking her cue. As always, when she stood in front of him, she was surprised he was so much taller. The smoothness of his outline, the slight overweight, didn't suggest height. He preceded her to the door and opened it for her. "I'm glad you find your off-duty time stimulating, Mrs. Markham."

"Oh, a sense of festivity every night," she said, and meant it.

2

That night, there were only Cora and one of the young men at dinner, and she didn't feel festive at all. She was probably tired. No one talked much, and afterwards they sat in front of some undemanding programmes on television. Cora said it was a good idea when Helen suggested retiring a bit earlier than usual, and came to her room about twenty minutes after they had all gone up.

"How are you, then?"

She was perched on the end of the bed almost before Helen had said sit down. She wore a pretty cotton robe which fell away from her arched knees. The thought of her being Mr. Jones's daughter brought a brief creep of sensation under Helen's skin.

"I'm all right." Matching informality with informality, Helen cast off her own robe and climbed into bed. She gave a little laugh into Cora's attentive face.

"What is it?" There was the ghost of a frown, as if Cora was searching the laugh for any hysteria content. But Helen had taken a deliberate decision to bend the unwritten rules.

"Only that—well, you really do have the advantage, don't you?"

"Meaning?" There was no expression on Cora's face.

"Meaning you know everything about me, Cora, but everything. And I know nothing whatsoever about you. To the point of downright unnaturalness, in each case. It's like the telly pundit, you know his tastes and his allergies and his marital score. And he doesn't even know you exist!"

"You know that about me, at least." Cora was smiling now.

"Yes. As a physical fact. Beyond that . . ."

"Beyond that, we none of us really know about anybody." Cora was all at once sombre. "I came to see how you were after what must have been an ordeal."

Off her own bat, or on a double check ordered by Mr. Jones? "Thank you, I'm all right."

"I'm glad."

How much purpose, for goodness' sake, was there in, or instead of, this personal concern? She decided to extend the new ground.

"You shouldn't be encouraging me to think about myself just now, should you?" *Myself?* Across the room she saw the curve of her bare shoulder in the cheval glass.

"You're too intelligent," said Cora, smiling again but her eyes colder, "to take it as encouragement. To say nothing of your instincts of self-preservation."

"Are we working tomorrow?"

"You have the weekend off." Cora stretched her legs, relaxed. She had probably been braced for more awkward questions or implications. "We aim for you to come here every weekend. You need to be yourself now and then."

"In case I really lose my mind?"

"Something like that, perhaps," said Cora, lazily smiling but offering Helen her sharpest vision yet of professional ruthlessness. She got off the bed and stopped at the door.

"Good night."

"Good night."

Helen heard the key turn in the lock.

3

Mrs. Gray always brought her tea and toast in her room. Next morning she said, "Mr. Jones will see you in the office at eleven."

Up till now the first appointment had been at nine o'clock, and in the big room under the pitched roof.

Helen used the extra time to get up and dress very slowly and carefully, savouring the luxury and trying to insulate it from her fears.

Mr. Jones poured her out a cup of coffee.

"Two days' leave. I hope you will relax inwardly as well, Mrs. Markham." He spoke to her now from across his desk. "The next session will be taxing."

"Of course. And I'm rested already. But it isn't—relaxation as one knew it—before—is it? Can it be?"

"No. But it's a question of the will." Mr. Jones got to his feet and moved slowly across to the window. *Will, discipline, intelligence, self-preservation.* Say them all, reflected Helen, loud and clear, and there would still be times of day which induced certain reactions, somewhere, however faintly, from an English bourgeois lifetime of associations. Seeing Mr. Jones as her employer in a dark suit, in the middle of the morning, she realized that the night before she had seen him as an attractive man.

"The will," repeated Mr. Jones, at the window, putting up his hand to lean there, but not disturbing the net curtain. "The will is what we must work on, as well as the essential skills. The stronger the will becomes, that is to say, the more biddable, the safer we are."

"Like sleeping with a baby in the house." She was quoting someone from the other world, remembering her hurt that she had never had the experience. "You still sleep, but never completely. You expect to be disturbed."

"You express it admirably, Mrs. Markham." Mr. Jones went back behind his desk, sat down and gazed at her. "We must always expect to be disturbed."

"I wonder if it's a state I shall be able to disacquire, when I've finished?"

"Don't wonder, Mrs. Markham, at least not yet. It's a luxury you can't afford."

They looked steadily into each other's eyes. Mr. Jones's eyes were unexpectedly large above his pale rounded cheeks. Not the ice-cold eyes of spy legend, but not warm, either. Had he sent Cora to her the night before? If only she could stop formulating internal questions for which there could be no answers. *Accept. Be passive where you can't be active. Conserve your strength.*

He had said that to her one morning, on one of his infrequent visits to the upstairs room.

"Now, before you go off duty, Mrs. Markham, is there anything you wish to ask me about next week?"

"Will Miss Jones have any visitors?"

"Not until one of us comes to bring you back here on Friday." She wondered if he had deliberately avoided the word *home*. "On the other afternoons, watch other people's visitors. Call on Mrs. Harvey and Mrs. Lambert."

"I will. Will you say something to the staff about no sugar and less milk?"

"I will. Now, you might like to go into the drawing-room, Mrs. Markham." Mr. Jones got up. Helen, despite her decision to try and give up profitless speculation, couldn't help wondering whether the polite obliqueness of his orders was the carrying out of a general directive to operators, or merely his personal style.

In the drawing-room Cora was lolling in an armchair, reading the paper. She took the outside pages and passed them without comment to Helen. Evidently she was her afternoon, rather than her morning, self. After lunch she went with Helen into the garden. They sat down eventually on a stone seat beside one of the paths, the sun warm on their faces. It was the first time she had felt the sun since the year before, since . . . The pang came, obediently, but she was more aware of that unaccustomed warmth on her face, the song of the birds. Cora said she helped Tom, The Laurels gardener, as often as she got the chance.

So ordinary an occupation in the case of a Jones was unimaginable. Helen realized she had imagined them dematerializing between assignments, and grinned at the thought.

"What is it?" asked Cora quickly.

"It's just that—well, life for me has taken a turn for the unusual. And I do, actually, have a rather unwieldy sense of humour."

Although Cora laughed quite a lot, in the afternoons and evenings, Helen suspected that she didn't have all that much sense of humour. She knew Mr. Jones had some. It was a quality which could be disguised, but not assumed.

"As long as you control it," said Cora.

"I'm sure I shall manage to do that. I'm grateful for the holiday, by the way."

As the hours went on, it seemed like a long one. There was so much time alone in her room, where she tried to acquire the sort of relaxed attitude counselled by Mr. Jones, but found a tension almost too sharp in the contrast between how she was and how she was soon to be. It was better at mealtimes and in the evening, when it was interesting to watch how the unsmiling work relationships between Cora and the young men became the usual exchanges of intelligent and mutually attractive young people. Not that Cora appeared to favour either of the two young men.

"*Appear*," said Helen aloud and savagely into her mirror before dinner on Sunday night. "*Appear*. It's all appear and appearances except for me . . ." She stopped abruptly, staring wide-eyed at her reflection in the soft lamplight. Thin pale face, grey-white hair, long white neck and bare white arms, what was behind their varying appearance?

"John," she whispered, "John," turning and looking round the shadow-laden room. But it wasn't the least part of an answer, and there was no other name to say.

At table, warmed with wine, stimulated and amused with conversation, she supposed that people in Mr. Jones's line of business might come to live quite happily in appearances. She herself seemed to be managing, but then she had had a good start.

She looked round the elegant table, across the quiver of the candles. Really, they were like people who had been invited to a house party and were fortunate enough to find one another agreeable.

CHAPTER 5

1

The large area of glass in the lounge at Hill House was double-glazed against the cold, and central heating radiators spread round the three sides of the huge bay. Yet even in March, when the sun shone, there were a few afternoon hours when the venetian blinds must be lowered and zebra stripes lay across the reclining figures.

On the coldly sunny afternoon when Helen was taken back
for her first full week in the nursing home and had been settled in her chair against the far wall between Mrs. Anthony
and Mrs. Charlesworth, she saw sections of Mr. Weston
through the slats of the blind as he passed the garden, and
that he had something white in his hand. When he reappeared, at just the time it would have taken him to slip an envelope into the pillar-box at the junction of the first side street,
he had nothing. The front door at Hill House had been kept
locked since a vague lady had once wandered out and been
found anxious hours later making sandcastles with some children on the beach, but keys were allocated to those few considered sufficiently responsible to be entrusted with them. Mr.
Weston must come into that category, for the front doorbell
hadn't rung and here he was, clearing his throat in the way
Helen already anticipated, taking a seat in the lounge. She
must make a note of it.

In her mind. And now she must hold all her observations in
her mind for four days. She was forbidden to have with her
anything Miss Jones wouldn't have, so while she sat and
watched she must also gather and retain the information she
would set down on paper as soon as she was back in her room
at The Laurels. She had told Mr. Jones about the inner visual
faculty which had once helped her in exams by enabling her
to recall the appearance of the pages on which information
was written, and they had given her exercises in reviving it.
Now, she must try to assemble her own pages in her head, and
hold them ready to set down. It was an uncomfortable and
frustrating process, but at least it was an occupation for those
times when there was nothing to hear and nothing to see except sleeping faces, something to set against the dangerous
possibility of falling asleep herself . . .

The door was opening from the dining-room, there were the
crockery sounds, the glimpses of nurses. Mr. Thomas craned
round to look at the clock, Miss Anthony got to her feet and
stood clasping her mother's hands. Helen stared at the contact,
reminding herself, as with Mr. Weston, that she must make no

assumptions as to directions in which observation was unnecessary, or suspicion absurd.

Miss Anthony laid her mother's hands in her lap. Mr. Weston was on his feet again, clearing his throat.

"Coming through?" he asked hoarsely of Mr. Thomas.

Mr. Thomas hove to his feet and took a couple of steps forwards. "Yes. Yes. Tea-time. Yes, I think I might . . ."

"I shan't be here tomorrow, Mother," said Miss Anthony, "but you'll see me on Friday."

"That will be very nice, dear. Give me a kiss."

"Tea . . . tea . . ." Mrs. Stoddart had got herself to her feet, and was eddying round in ever unsteadier circles. Helen held her hands together in her lap, to combat her instinct to catch Mrs. Stoddart before she fell.

Nurse Jackie just did it, and led Mrs. Stoddart off. The words "infuse" and "caddy" drifted back, and Helen was assailed from one direction against which neither she nor Mr. Jones had prepared a defence: she wanted to laugh, so strongly she must dissipate it in a sneezing cough. But it was probably nerves rather than amusement.

"All right, dear?"

Nurse Jackie was back to help her, and to look at her not quite so vaguely as usual, because of the uncharacteristic noise she had just made.

"All right . . . yes . . ."

They moved off across the lounge and near the dining-room door the nurse left Miss Jones to carry on alone. Helen sat down, still holding her hands together in her lap, this time to control their trembling. If she was in danger from laughter she was in danger from everything.

"It's been a beautiful day," observed Miss Protheroe. "I'm looking forward to the sunset."

Miss Duncan sniffed. "There probably won't be one. It's going dull."

Helen picked up Miss Duncan's napkin ring and stroked it. It was made of china, decorated with roses. Miss Jones, Mrs. Anthony and Miss Protheroe had Hill House plastic rings, their names on little labels. Miss Duncan started to put her hand out towards Helen, then withdrew it.

"Yes," said Miss Protheroe. "I really don't think she'll do it any harm."

"I know that, I know that." Miss Duncan drew a sharp breath. Something in her eyes briefly blurred their incision. Helen put the ring back beside Miss Duncan's plate. Miss Duncan waited until she had had a sip of tea before moving the ring slightly closer to her.

"Very pretty," said Miss Jones.

"Yes. Very pretty." Miss Protheroe smiled at her, as if Miss Jones was normal. It could only be because Miss Protheroe was an instinctively nice person. *Couldn't it?* Once again Helen wiped her hands down her bib.

That tea-time there was no tart commentator.

"Mrs. Wellington must be having tea out," commented Miss Protheroe.

"There have to be some compensations in the most wretched existence." Miss Duncan was over her moment of weakness, if she had suffered one.

"What did you say?" enquired Mrs. Anthony. She was hard of hearing but her requests for repetition were intermittent and apparently arbitrary.

"Mrs. Wellington is out for tea today," said Miss Protheroe, a little more loudly. Helen was pleased to see her smile at Mrs. Anthony as scrupulously as she had smiled at Miss Jones.

"Mrs. Wellington's got a daughter, hasn't she?" asked Mrs. Anthony. Her expression was unvaryingly amiable.

"That's right, dear."

"I don't . . . that is, I think . . . a brother," faltered Miss Jones.

"Yes, and you have a brother, Miss Jones," agreed Miss Protheroe.

Nurse Jackie came round the table and put Helen's cup between her hands. The main course was sausage and beans, cold and greasy on the plate long before Miss Jones could have been expected to finish it.

2

Time was of an unfamiliar order, generous, steady, slow. Perhaps as time had once been everywhere, before trains and planes and cars, when women sat day after day on the same sofa, sewing through uneventful afternoons . . .

Even such superficial speculation was to be discouraged. Sitting in the lounge after tea, staring, between her rounds of observation, at Miss Protheroe's sunset and then at dark red curtains, Helen planned her night. She sat on in the lounge through a quiz and a situation comedy on television, through the return of Mrs. Wellington. Mrs. Wellington came in, slightly flushed and temporarily released from boredom, looking like a visitor until a nurse took her fur hat and coat away and she sat down without bothering to raise her hands to her flattened hair. Helen felt a pang of pity, before remembering that Mrs. Wellington might be the one person who deserved none.

"Hello," said Mrs. Anthony.

"Did you have a good time, dearie?" Mrs. Stoddart leaned towards Mrs. Wellington. Miss Protheroe showed no awareness of the return, but once the curtains were drawn she looked mostly down at her lap. Miss Welch stared at the newcomer, terrified, and then in equal panic at Mrs. Anthony and Mrs. Stoddart as they spoke. Mr. Thomas smoked reflectively, in one of his phases where he showed no reaction to external events. Mrs. Barker looked interested and Miss Duncan didn't raise her eyes from her book.

Mrs. Wellington's eyes were already closed. Helen wondered if she had imagined the slight colour in her face. "Yes. It's not worth it, though, when one has to come back here."

Miss Jones got up and drifted towards the door. She used the arm of Mrs. Wellington's chair to help herself along, touching the hand lying there. Mrs. Wellington opened her eyes, but lazily. Helen stared through them.

"Oh, you." Mrs. Wellington shut her eyes. Her hand was cool and dry. Helen went out of the lounge and into the cloakroom, which had three lavatory cubicles, three wash-basins, and a chair with a cork seat. The cubicles were empty and she sat down on the chair, allowing herself the one possible respite, which was to cease to stare.

Water chattered in the pipes, and no one came. Helen closed her eyes and began to arrange the first page of her report. *Mr. Weston got rid of the white object I have no doubt he was carrying (there is a pillar-box at the first corner and the timing would be right). He reappeared without the doorbell ringing so must have a key. Miss Protheroe looks at everyone as if they are all there. Miss Duncan reacted to my handling of her napkin ring in a way I would find it hard to believe was feigned. But she is probably the cleverest person at Hill House. Mrs. Wellington is either innocent or phenomenally well disciplined: I touched her hand when her eyes were closed and she opened them without any other bodily reaction . . .*

The door creaked and Helen opened hers. Miss Protheroe did not appear to change her bearing in any way. But of course she had immediately seen Miss Jones.

"Hello, dear." Miss Protheroe smiled, went briefly into one of the cubicles. When she came out she washed her hands without glancing in the mirror above the basins. She held out a hand to Helen, small, red, and rough. A hand that looked as if it had done a lot of work.

"Are you coming?"

"I'm very well, thank you," said Miss Jones, staring through her.

"All right, you sit there, then," said Miss Protheroe, after an uncomfortable few seconds of looking at Helen as if she was Helen. She flitted out, her feet silent on the tiles.

Helen moved her chair so that it was half behind a jutting piece of wall, and she might not be spotted at once. Miss Welch burst in and went straight to the mirror, where she stared tragically at her image. Braced for at least a scream, Helen let the big black handbag Miss Jones always carried fall to the floor. But Miss Welch turned towards her looking neither more nor less wild than she normally did.

"I thought I'd sit . . ." said Helen, not expecting a response. She was already sure that Miss Welch (the Miss Welch character?) spoke only when authoritatively encouraged or really in need. Now Miss Welch dived into a cubicle where she made much noisy play with paper. Helen froze in the act of bending over to retrieve her handbag. Would Miss Jones pick it up? Miss Welch might be the one person to be suspicious if she did . . . Helen felt a wave of irrational but energizing fury against Mr. Jones, sitting in his grey-green office and appointing people to impossible and perilous activities. She got up from her seat, ignoring the bag, and stared into the mirror. As always, during the seconds in which she allowed her eyes to focus, she was aghast at what she saw. Good. Behind her, Miss Welch dashed out of the lavatory cubicle and out of the cloakroom, apparently without a further glance at Miss Jones. Helen sat down again just as Sister Wendy came in with Mrs. Stoddart.

"So there you are, chick! One place as good as another, I suppose. Here we are, then."

Sister Wendy picked up the handbag and put it on to Helen's lap, guiding her fingers to the handle.

"My bag," said Miss Jones.

"Yes, your bag. You hold on to it!"

"Will. Yes."

"What've you got in there?" Sister Wendy gestured at the bag.

"Got a key!" Helen opened the bag, clumsily, and poked out the large key from among the unrelated and inapplicable objects which Miss Jones preferred to carry.

"That's a fine key!" As always, Helen was aware of Sister Wendy's alertness and energy. Normally, these qualities would have been invigorating. Now . . .

"All right, Mrs. Stoddart?" called Sister Wendy. "Want any help?"

"I'm all right, dear, if you'll just put the kettle on."

The lavatory flushed. "Going back now?" suggested Sister Wendy to Miss Jones. Helen shut the bag on the key and got slowly to her feet. Sister Wendy held the door for her and she wandered back to the lounge. Hot drinks were being handed out, sign that Miss Jones's bedtime was imminent and that the most potentially fruitful part of Helen's assignment lay ahead.

But first, as Mr. Jones had stressed, she should try to sleep, and to sleep at nine o'clock in the evening was as yet the order she found it hardest to obey. She was braced for perpetual vigilance, and anyway she wasn't used to sleeping at the time which for more than a decade had meant relaxing with John after dinner, and then, when she joined Reddington Rep, being on stage. But she feigned sleep, when they brought Mrs. Barker up, snuggling the bedclothes high round her face, forcing her body to go limp when she heard the welcome words "Good night, then, Miss Jones," from the doorway.

She had always been able to alert an inner alarm clock, and at Hill House she set it for 1 A.M. She must have slept, because when she drifted, slipperless, across the carpet to the mantel-piece and the clock there, she saw by the triangle of moonlight at the top of the curtains that it was five minutes to. She went over to the window, widening the white glow to a bright searchlight which lay across Mrs. Barker's humped and motionless bed. It was a relief at least to be free of net curtain.

The moon rode in a brown circle of frost, the roof of the extended lounge below shone black under its thin cold layer, she could see the sea horizon glinting in the distance, a darker grey than the sky. There was no wind, no sound. Close to the glass she felt the sharpness of the night on her nose and chin, but Hill House was well heated, for which she was grateful—Miss Jones did not pause to don dressing-gown and slippers before setting off on her travels.

Mrs. Harvey and Mrs. Lambert were across the landing. Their door, not properly latched, opened with ease.

Here there was no moonlight, only the grey curtained oblong of the window. It took Helen a few motionless seconds to make out the beds along the walls. From one of them came heavy rhythmic snoring, varying only in volume as she stood looking and listening. She turned to the silent bed, put her hand out, let it alight on hair and forehead, trail softly down temple and cheek. Cool, papery. Very soft breathing here . . .

It was so appallingly sudden, the vice on her wrist, the light in her eyes. Surely even a real Miss Jones would have registered shock? The other hand was pressing the bell whose flex lay across the bedside locker. The face, beneath sparse untidy grey hair, was fierce, thin and yellow.

Helen whimpered, letting her face crumple, and the grip relaxed.

"Why can't they lock you up?" demanded a voice which clearly knew what it was saying.

Helen turned away, rubbing her wrist. In the other bed the snoring continued. A sickening smell was advancing across the room. Helen, swallowing down her reaction, examined an ugly vase on top of a chest of drawers, then sat down in the armchair at the foot of the sleeper's bed. She stared through the angry woman opposite, now settling slightly back on her pillows. The snoring ended in a pig's whistle, just as the night nurse Helen had already encountered came into the room.

"Miss Jones! Oh dear. They did say, but we hoped . . ."

"It really is too bad." The woman she had wakened was sitting forward. "Can't you lock her in?"

"I don't think, Mrs. Harvey . . . I'm very sorry. But she's harmless."

"Nothing that gropes for your face in the night is harmless."

"No. I'm sorry." Nurse Sandra wrinkled her nose. "I'll see to your sister while I'm here."

She pulled the clothes back from the other bed and Helen had to swallow again, hard.

"Dear me!" said the nurse, swinging into a clearly familiar routine. Mrs. Harvey lay back now, her gaunt profile to the ceiling. No one took any notice of Miss Jones, until Mrs. Lambert sat up, saw her, and held out her arms with a smile. On a quick glance the ash-blonde curls and round pink smiling face suggested childhood. But as Helen stared into the blue eyes which moved with childlike delight over herself, the nurse, the room, it was obvious that this child was middle-aged.

Mrs. Lambert had snuggled down and was gazing admiringly across at her sister.

"Get rid of her when you go, will you?" The waxen face nodded at Helen.

"Of course I will. Now, Mrs. Harvey, up we go!"

The nurse put her arms under the bedclothes. Mrs. Harvey put her arms round the nurse's neck in a gesture it must once have hurt her spirit to make. The nurse heaved upwards—and it seemed to Helen that a rag doll was tossed lightly over the nurse's shoulder. There was so little of Mrs. Harvey: each leg ended above the knee.

Helen got to her feet and blundered out of the room. The child's laughter could be heard until the other bedroom door was closed.

Everyone makes a mistake somewhere, and that was mine. It isn't that I did anything out of character, but I did it for the wrong reason, because I, Helen Markham, was affected.

It was as bad as any half-hour of her life, as bad as first knowing John was leaving, that her mother was dying. The nurse briefly in the doorway, saying "All right, then, Miss Jones?" without interest—that helped the immediate anxiety, but it didn't help the aches and pains of her spirit, the unleashed pity for all created things which had her tossing about the bed until the only remedy was to get up and carry on with her job.

She went first to stare at herself in the mirror. She had told Cora that she could assume a role only from the inside, but now for the first time she watched Helen Markham and her distress disappearing, she saw them in the moonlit gloom shrinking down behind and inside Miss Jones's anxious gaze as if she was locking them away. And she found that was what she wanted. It could be that the assumption of a new persona was like a tranquillizing drug or a lobotomy, continuously postponing self-confrontation . . .

But not self-indulgence. She must never begin to feel she had totally mastered her will. As if in acknowledgement of the constant danger of weakness she made a Miss Jones groping movement between the dressing-table and the bed, then went out on to the landing.

Just in time to see a female figure, wraith-like in its long pale gown and the dim light, flitting round a corner out of sight.

As waveringly, Miss Jones followed, her lack of purpose foiling Helen Markham's sense of it, so that when she turned into the long corridor which ran off the landing there was no one to be seen.

The first door was ajar and Miss Jones pushed it open, standing irresolute on the threshold. By the dim, sparsely set passage lights it was just possible for Helen to make out upholstered chairs and low tables haphazard round the room. There was good carpet under her bare feet and the television screen winked at her as her eyes adjusted to the gloom. For their leisure moments the staff at Hill House were well looked after. The room was empty.

Across the corridor, the door marked *Matron* was shut and locked. The door beyond it was shut, but the handle turned easily. The ceiling light immediately outside showed her more quickly than she had made out the sitting-room the two beds with the two sleeping women. She thought one was Nurse Jackie but as she stood staring the other woman murmured and threw an arm towards the ceiling and Helen went back into the corridor, closing the door almost silently behind her. She waited for a moment, as thank heaven Miss Jones might wait, but listening, and after a count of fifty, she opened the door opposite—and bit her lips on a smile. The shrill white light from the bedside lamp threw a spotlight on to Mrs. Armitage the deputy matron, asleep on her back with a book open on the rise of her bosom. There was a pincurl to each side of her rosy cheeks, one plump hand still lay on the edge of the book, a radio muttered softly from behind the lamp. Feeling Miss Jones a moth to a candle, settling more firmly into the vacuousness of her expression as if it was a mask, Helen prepared to move forward. But the deputy matron sighed, moved a hand up to her throat, which she began to caress, and Miss Jones turned and drifted out of the room.

Four more doors now, one locked, one disclosing a bathroom and lavatory, one seen to contain two more sleeping women but no drifting wraith, the last at the very end of the

corridor, opposite a frosted window. As Helen put her hand
out to the knob it turned from the other side and the door
began slowly to open. Afterwards she was glad she had been
subjected to such a test, because she knew she had passed it,
that none of her screaming panic was anywhere near her anxious Miss Jones face.

Mrs. Stoddart was wavering in the dark gap, advancing her
face close to Helen's, smiling horribly.

"Shall we have some tea, dearie, some tea?" She put her
hand out and stroked Helen's arm. She began to laugh.

CHAPTER 6

1

"Yes, we had two wanderers the night before last." Sister
Wendy turned her smiling gaze from Mr. Jones to Helen.
"Miss Jones met Mrs. Stoddart in the wee-est of the small
hours, coming out of our little staff kitchen. Do you know,
Mrs. Stoddart had actually put the kettle on! Miss Jones must
have had an instinct to join her for a cuppa. Mustn't you,
lovey?" Helen forced herself to smile uncertainly into the
bright eyes. "There can still be a feeling . . . All right, dear?"
Sister Wendy had turned her attention to Mrs. Stoddart, who
was leaning towards them in vague inquiry. "Sometimes she
wants more than make-believe, even now." She patted Mrs.
Stoddart's hand, then turned back to Mr. Jones. "Your sister
seems to be settling in all right, Mr. Jones. She wanders about
a bit, yes, but people are very . . . She's made quite a friend
of our Mrs. Roberts in the kitchen. And she doesn't have to
keep going to the lavvy like poor Mr. Thomas and Miss Welch
and so many of them. We'll do very well together." Sister

Wendy bounced to her feet, pushing back the hair which had escaped her cap. "But I mustn't stay chattering here all afternoon, tempting as it is." With a cheerful smile at Mr. Jones and Helen she set off across the room.

"Nice girl. Nice Wendy."

"Yes, indeed."

She thought the response was automatic, and perhaps the lifting of her hand into his lap, without looking, as he gazed lazily round the room. But for a sharp second she was aware of the dry white hand round hers, stroking it, lacing the fingers, before she too resumed the familiar circuit, consciously diverting sensation from hand to eye and exhilarated by the speed of her reaction.

The blinds were down in the lounge but partly open, and a striped submarine peace lay over the room. A band of light covered Mrs. Wellington's closed eyes. Miss Welch was being addressed earnestly and softly and without response, by a middle-aged girl who Mr. Jones had ascertained in casual conversation was her sister. Mr. Thomas was dozing, Miss Duncan was talking, in an emphatic exchange, to a woman who looked and sounded much like herself. Mrs. Charlesworth was staring into space and Miss Protheroe between the slats of the blind. Mrs. Wayne-Jenkins could be seen intermittently beyond the window. Even in winter and a cold spring, Mrs. Wayne-Jenkins walked before tea-time round and round the garden—one of the nurses had told Miss Jones, as in kindly charade they had told her other things. Miss Jones and Mrs. Anthony, sitting across from the enormous window, faced the major part of her circuit, and nearly every time Mrs. Wayne-Jenkins battled past, Mrs. Anthony exclaimed in surprise that there was yet another lady on the lawn. The only exception to Mrs. Wayne-Jenkins's routine was when she had a visitor and patronized the lounge. And created a little difficulty with regard to chairs.

Those who sat regularly in the lounge had, with use, established their rights to certain seats, which were respected even by the feebler-minded. The previous afternoon Mrs. Wayne-Jenkins had led her visitor to the best-placed empty chairs, and there had been a disturbance when the regular oc-

cupiers came in to sit down, the brighter spectators combining
to aid the dispossessed. Order had been restored in the form
of Mrs. Wayne-Jenkins and her visitor retiring indignantly to
the big settee in the hall. In the lounge, the legitimate incum-
bents of the chairs gradually subsided as the upheaval subsided
around them. Helen had been irresistibly reminded of a disturbance in a hen run; the squawking, the wing-flapping, the
advancing and retracting of beaks, the slow settling of ruffled
feathers, the softening of the clucking to a mollified murmur . . .

She was hard put to it not to drowse, sitting still as she must
while Mr. Jones sat beside her holding her hand, making her
feel that for a few moments at least he had taken over. The
night had been fruitless but it had been active, in and out of
moonlit bedrooms where whistles, snores and groans arose
from motionless or threshing bodies and where lockers were
pathetically empty of personal possessions, sitting a half hour
with the nurse on duty, in and out of rooms again . . . And
the fruitless morning had been spent largely in kitchen and
cloakroom.

"Look, Mary," exclaimed Mrs. Anthony at her side. "Another lady on the lawn!"

Miss Anthony and her mother were holding hands on the
arm of Mrs. Anthony's chair. Helen, looking at the pale expressionless face, wondered what sort of a life the girl led. Within
the unattractive frame of her lank hair, Miss Anthony was not
bad-looking. Unmemorable, though. Not to be recognized if
encountered out of context, or on the other hand one could
imagine that every ninth or tenth young woman passed in the
street was Miss Anthony. No distinguishing features. But perhaps it was simply that every resident of the lounge at Hill
House was as idiosyncratic as a character from Dickens, each
one just falling into caricature like an illustration by Phiz . . .

Mr. Weston came in, clearing his throat, and Mrs. Wellington
opened her eyes wide and stared at him until he was settled in
the comparatively unfavourable position which was the pen-
alty for spending half the day in other places. Helen tried to
think what it was which made her see Mr. Weston as different

from the rest of them. It seemed absurd, but she thought it was a sense of purpose. Or simply that this was a quality so apparently lacking in everyone else . . .

She had one or two ideas she would like to pass over to Mr. Jones. Now, not waiting for another forty-eight hours. The dossier might be negative, but it got longer and longer, and more and more unwieldy to hold in her head. She felt her fingertips, as if involuntarily, press briefly into the palm of his hand. It seemed to be precisely then that he said, putting her hand back in her lap,

"Well, sweetheart, it's not a bad sort of a day. How would you like to go down to the sea for an ice-cream?"

"What is it, Julian, I don't think I can . . ."

He was helping her to her feet. Sister Wendy was back beside them.

"There is all of an hour before tea," said Mr. Jones. "And it's the warmest day of the year. I think I'll take her down to the sea for an ice-cream. If you don't think it will spoil her appetite."

"If it does we shan't worry." Sister Wendy gave him her radiant smile. "I don't expect it will, though. Miss Jones enjoys her food. I'll pop up for her coat."

"I wish you'd take me." Mrs. Wellington hadn't bothered to open her eyes.

"I would, Mrs. Wellington." Mr. Jones spoke gently. "Only you know it's not encouraged to take other people's—"

"Any excuse!" She gave him an angry look, but kept her eyes open until she had absorbed his smile.

"I'm sorry."

"That comes cheap." Mrs. Wellington made a sort of angular nestling movement into her chair. When Mr. Jones and his sister reached the door Miss Protheroe raised a hand in salute without turning from her contemplation of the sky.

"Here we are!" In the hall Sister Wendy helped Helen into her coat, helped Mr. Jones get her down the steps and into the front seat of the car. "You'd better have these, lovey." She put a handful of paper tissues in Helen's lap.

"Efficient young lady. All set, then, sweetheart? Off we go, then." He slammed the car door, went round and got in the other side. Mrs. Wayne-Jenkins, about to cross the drive as they moved forward, glared at Helen, then smiled impatiently at Mr. Jones. They nosed between the posts.

"Let's make it Boscombe, dear," said Mr. Jones in his cheerful good-brother voice. Helen didn't respond. It wasn't necessary, and anyway she was busy a few moments subduing that self which found it hard to accept the fact that despite being alone with Mr. Jones in a moving car, looking out on people and places which had nothing to do with her job, she was as much on duty as if she was still in her chair in the lounge at Hill House. When he drew up at the head of Boscombe pier she stayed slumped in her seat, staring ahead.

"Here we are, then."

Out of the corner of her eye she saw there was a sweet-shop.

"Open the window," she asked him, quietly.

He leaned across her, and as the handle turned she was aware, and with a briefly painful sensation, of the soft fresh air, the sound of unconcerned voices, the smell of the sea.

"I'll get you ready before I have my hands full." He arranged the tissues over her chest, tucking one into the neck of her dress. She made no move to assist him. "Shan't be a tick!"

She didn't watch him in the shop. He was back almost at once with two pink cornets and put one of them into her hand through the window. He resumed his seat beside her, confirming the volume.

"Nice of you to keep me company."

"I like ice-cream. How are you?"

"As well as can be expected." A large blob of ice-cream fell on to the tissues. She really didn't know whose accident it was, hers or Miss Jones's.

"Good," he said.

She told him about Monday night and about Tuesday, which had yielded nothing. When she had finished he made no comment, but invited hers.

"I'm personally satisfied," she said slowly, "that Mrs. Harvey and Mrs. Lambert are exactly what they seem."

"But Mrs. Lambert has legs for walking?"

"She has. But you told me yourself she never left the room and unless she was in professional cahoots with Mrs. Harvey that eagle eye would be the last one under which to be other than one's apparent self." The relief of being able to think aloud was enormous. But she was aware, to her amusement, that she was feeling slightly sulky with Mr. Jones, because he was ultimately responsible for the fact that it was the only concession she was able to make to this sunny afternoon by the sea. "I mean," she said, "would you do it that way?"

"Not if there were slightly easier ways, and of course there are. Yes. Leave the Misses Harvey and Lambert for the time being." She felt him turn towards her. She realized that she hadn't looked at him since he had first come into the lounge at Hill House an hour ago.

"You said you wouldn't be coming."

"I changed my mind. Did you rest between visiting those two ladies, and following Mrs. Stoddart?"

"I lay down for half an hour." She cut off her harsh laugh, but she would probably have done that anyway.

"Any instincts?"

She couldn't really sulk, it would be ridiculous. "I get a feeling that there's something about Mr. Weston. I don't know what. Just something. But perhaps that's simply because I saw him go out and post a letter. Which would be no reason. So I do have a feeling. Perhaps it's just that everyone else is so aimless. And . . ."

"Yes?"

She had finished the ice-cream, and dabbed ineptly at the tissues.

"All right, dear. Let me."

He took her hands in turn and wiped them, then put a tissue to her lips. As he took it away it was the only time, on a conscious decision, that she looked at him, and as Helen Markham. He looked back at her, motionless through several seconds, and she was aware, not of hope, not of pleasure, but of a sort of stirring of her anticipation of the future, so that she glimpsed very briefly that it was after all still composed of layers of sensation and experience.

"You do uncannily well," he said, turning away.

"I have that talent. I wish I'd gone on the stage."

He accorded the remark a few moments' silence.

"You were going to say something, I think."

"Yes . . ." She had half hoped he had missed the attempt. "It's the vaguest, most unsupported of feelings. About Mrs. Barker. She's very sharp, and a couple of times, when I've gone into the bedroom, she's been sort of pottering about on her Zimmer near her bed and there's no doubt she's jumped and turned at least her head quickly and looked . . . well, guilty. This of course I know is why she probably can't be. Then when she sees it's only Miss Jones, she relaxes. But I do feel she's hiding *something*. I also feel certain that she really is crippled with arthritis. Well, I suppose your target could be. Could be at Hill House for that very reason."

He said softly, "Of course. Anything more?"

"No."

His left hand was resting on the driving wheel and his watch showed under the light grey cuff. "Tea-time?"

"You're right. We'll go back."

He was no longer calling her Mrs. Markham. The shudder had gone through her before she could prevent it.

"What is it?" They were both looking straight ahead.

"Only the goose on the grave. Me, in other words." *Me?* "I mean, the absence of me. The feeling that perhaps I don't exist. You can't call me anything."

"I would advise against philosophical speculation even when you are off duty. And at the moment you are not." She could hardly have expected anything gentler. He leaned across to close her window and her heart sank. "Have an easy night tonight."

He started the engine. They didn't speak again until they drew up outside the front door of Hill House.

"Now, sweetheart," said Mr. Jones, "you sit here and I'll come round and help you to get out."

When he opened the door she heard a blackbird singing its joyous recognition of the spring. It made her want to leap out of the car and run, run and run to exhaust her body until it matched her mind. The prospect for a few seconds seemed so supremely enticing she nearly did it.

2

Mr. Jones handed her over in the hall, and Nurse Jackie took her straight into the dining-room. Mrs. Barker wasn't there, and wasn't there either during the evening. Otherwise nothing seemed different from usual. About half an hour before the hot drink was due she went and sat in the downstairs cloakroom, where her only client was Mr. Corlett, from whose courteous demeanour no jot was taken off by the setting for their encounter. Like Miss Protheroe, he treated Miss Jones as if she was Helen, and so in a way did Sister Wendy on their way upstairs, only she was really talking to herself.

"You'll find Mrs. Barker in bed," said Sister Wendy, waiting while Miss Jones's fitful progress caught up with her own. "The poor lady seemed very unlike herself this afternoon and asked to be taken up while you were out with your brother. Oops-a-daisy, lovey. She didn't seem to have any sort of a new pain, and she doesn't look ill, but she obviously wanted to go and lie down so we took her up."

Mrs. Barker wasn't in bed when Sister Wendy opened the door, she was sitting on the edge and leaning awkwardly forward to reach into her locker. She pulled hastily back, her eyes full of pain, but Helen had seen fear in them as well.

Steadying her charge, Sister Wendy strode forward. "What is it, dear? D'you want something?"

"No, thank you." Mrs. Barker now was quite calm. "Help me back into bed, will you?"

With some difficulty Sister Wendy did so. "Do you want to read, lovey?"

"Thank you, I can reach my book."

"Right you are, then."

Sister Wendy was turning away, but Mrs. Barker suddenly put out her hand. Helen wavered across the room to her own bed and stood beside it, staring at Mrs. Barker and the nurse.

"What is it, lovey?"

Mrs. Barker increased her pressure on Sister Wendy's arm, until the young woman brought her head down close to the bed.

"I just wanted to say . . . You're a good girl, and kind. Thank you for looking after me."

It was the first time Helen had seen Sister Wendy discomfited. A flush suffused her face.

"Go along with you, Mrs. Barker! It's always a pleasure, anyway, as far as *you're* concerned."

"Is it? Is it really?" Mrs. Barker was briefly eager. Then she lay back on her pillow and her face was bleak. "Well, I'm grateful."

"That's all right." Sister Wendy straightened up. "I shouldn't read tonight if I were you. I should go to sleep." She turned towards Helen's bed. "All right, Miss Jones?"

Helen was unbuttoning her dress, discovering with her fingers a stiff patch of dried ice-cream.

"All right, yes . . ."

"All right, then. I'll look in later. Good night, Miss Jones. Mrs. Barker."

"Good night." Mrs. Barker lay motionless for a few moments after Sister Wendy had closed the door, then sat up, looked hard at Miss Jones, who was drifting about the room showing no awareness that she was other than alone, and again reached into her locker. She lifted a book on to the bed, opened it, and began to write. Helen, spine and scalp tingling with the excitement of the irregular, finished undressing under the tent of her nightgown, made much of washing her face and cleaning her teeth, got into bed and lay down facing Mrs. Barker.

There was the occasional rapid glance towards her. After perhaps fifteen minutes Sister Wendy put her head round the door, and again Helen saw the fear in Mrs. Barker's face and the uncharacteristic guarded look with which it was quickly replaced. The pen was out of sight.

"So you are reading after all, Mrs. Barker."

"Only for a few moments. I'm all right, Sister, I'll put my light out."

"Very well, then. Miss Jones all tucked up and serene? Good night, both of you."

The light went out overhead, and now there was only the small cone of Mrs. Barker's private illumination, directed downwards on to her like a miniature spotlight. And now Mr. Jones's agent had the advantage. In the concentrated light Helen saw clearly every movement of the fingers, steady across the page. After another ten or fifteen minutes, Mrs. Barker closed the book, stowed it back in her locker, put the light out and lay down.

The moon was full and after a few moments Helen could still make out the ruined profile staring at the ceiling, the eyes opening, closing, opening again. Suddenly Mrs. Barker sat up, turning towards Helen and probing her face so searchingly that Helen, the sweat creeping over her body, staring back because she must not suddenly close her eyes or look away, realized she could never say of the job Mr. Jones had given her that the worst was over.

"Don't look at me, dear," said Mrs. Barker at last, more gently than Helen had ever heard her speak.

She lay back again, sighing. Helen, for a moment rendered achingly sad, had consciously to restore her sense of danger.

3

She was dog-tired, but she lay awake for at least an hour before deciding that Mrs. Barker was either asleep or intending to sleep, and that she could do likewise. She was confident anyway, now, of waking up at the slightest sound her neighbour made.

But she suddenly knew, despite seeming to go from one waking thought to another, that for the first time at Hill House she had been sleeping heavily, too heavily to hear every sound. Also that she had not woken naturally. From this unaccustomed deep sleep there was a short climb back to full awareness, and she lay for a few moments, on her back where she found herself, before turning her head.

Mrs. Barker too was lying on her back, as she had been lying when Helen had last looked towards her, except that the hand nearer Helen was hanging down towards the floor. She was moaning, and the silhouette of her upper body, distinguishable in the moonlight, rose and fell. It was the only part of her which moved, until she began to speak and Helen saw her lips moving, and the serrated shadow on the wall behind her. Mrs. Barker said, "forgive-me-God-forgive-me" over and over again.

Then the monochrome picture with its two small points of movement changed. Mrs. Barker, gasping dreadfully, tried to lift her head from the pillow, but fell back. It was then Helen noticed the dark patches on the pale sheet and on the grey carpet under Mrs. Barker's dangling fingers. She wasn't thinking Miss Jones or Mrs. Markham as she lurched out of bed. The toes of one foot went straight into a warm sticky substance and she heard herself gasp and retch. She leaned forward and pulled the cord of Mrs. Barker's little light, and the black patches turned bright red. Mrs. Barker's weatherbeaten face was waxen yellow, and her other arm hung down the far side of the bed.

Helen pressed the bell between the beds several times, then climbed back into her own, protecting her blood-stained foot so that it came into contact with nothing before it touched her sheets. She curled up on her side, facing the window, thinking of the stack of men's handkerchiefs in her top drawer, one of which she could even by now have pulled tight on a bleeding wrist. She clasped her hands together against her noisy racing heart. If they didn't come, what would she do? What should she do? For the first time she recognized the starkly conflicting ethics. Miss Jones wouldn't have done anything, but she wasn't Miss Jones. And could anyone anyway say what Miss Jones would have done? A docile horse in one of Dorothy Sayers's crime novels had gone berserk when someone had tried to ride it past the spot where it had witnessed the violent shedding of blood . . .

"Forgive-me-God-forgive-me . . ."

The voice whispered relentlessly on. Helen added her own inner voice, and more. *Lord, hear our prayer, hers and mine.*

Mrs. Barker gave a dreadful broken cry, and as the door opened Helen was retching again, and must choke it down.

She saw the overhead light through her eyelids and the nurse shrieked. Night nurse Hazel it must be, the fat pale one. She tried, and failed, to imagine that casually good-natured face. Oh, why hadn't she put her handkerchiefs out, at least? Because of her blood-stained toes, that was why. Because she had acted by Mr. Jones's ethics. Let them not look in her bed, yet. Oh, let them not do anything but save Mrs. Barker. She could hear the ripping of cloth. The bell was pressed in an SOS pattern.

She didn't know how many people were eventually in the room. Two or three times she thought feet hovered near her, but it was known that when Miss Jones slept, she slept soundly.

The voices grew more subdued, the feet more frantic. Then there were the sounds of awkward movement, cautionary exclamations, a bump, grunts of achievement. Feet off carpet and on to floorboards. Silence. Then people hovering again, someone saying,

"Oh God, what about Miss Jones? D'you think . . . I mean . . ." and someone answering, "I know, it does seem sort of . . . But she's fast asleep and there's no earthly reason to disturb her." This was the deputy matron. "Clear the worst of it up, Hazel, will you, then when she comes to there'll be nothing to upset her. She'll be much more upset if we wake her and move her."

There was a sobbing murmur.

"I know, dear. It's a terrible thing. To reach such despair. But if she can be saved, they'll save her. Now, clear up will you, right away. Get one of the other girls to help you if you'd rather."

"No, I can manage. I'm sorry, Matron." Helen heard a gulping sound.

"Nothing to be sorry about. Now, I must go and see . . ."

A few moments later the sounds began again—rustling,

grunting, scrubbing. Helen was hardly aware of her body, cramped into paralysis because of what it might reveal if she gave it any grace at all, she was no more than a painfully tuned mind, able to register and process sounds. The sound of feet going to and from the hand-basin, of water slapping up and down the sides of a pail.

"That'll have to do."

She was grateful for the clue in the defiant words, and for the words which came next, from very close beside her, "Well, Miss Jones, you're having a good night's sleep, if no one else is."

She wasn't unaware of her body, she wanted to cough and she could no longer control the trembling of her shoulders. The only good sensation of the night was the sudden dusk on her eyelids, the sound of feet once more on floorboards, the closing of the door.

She lay for perhaps half an hour, very gently and gradually refamiliarizing herself with her arms and legs, her stomach muscles, her neck and hands.

When she eventually got out of bed, she was supple enough to speed straight to the basin and wash her foot. It would have been easier, if more horrible, had they not cleaned up and she could merely have waded deeper. She sped back to the bed with a face-cloth, peered between the sheets and washed the mercifully small stained area where her foot had lain. Only then did she walk round Mrs. Barker's bed on the damp carpet and, with another prayer, open the locker. Mrs. Barker might have found the pressures of espionage too great . . . of betrayal . . . But to write in a book . . . Didn't spies swallow telltale papers, let alone refrain from adding to them? If the book wasn't there she wouldn't know whether her job was half-done, or whether she had merely eliminated a suspect.

The book was there.

Helen sat down on the edge of the bare mattress and opened the book on her knees. She tried to calm herself, to fit herself to take in what she would read, telling herself that the smallest gesture, the knocking of the book to the floor, would be enough to put her back into character, and that the warning of a hand on the doorknob would give her the time.

It was a hard-backed exercise book, blank except for the first few pages, which were closely written in a feeble hand. The writing began at the top of the first page, without any heading.

I am considered to be a stable personality, and so they have told me the truth. They have told me that I shall never get better than I am now, that on the contrary I shall gradually and steadily get worse . . .

Time was perilous and precious, but she had to stop. Anyway, the few lines had told her enough. She sat there shivering, hugging herself against the desolation. It eased at last into a sense of shame for the determined depths of her own unhappiness.

She looked down once again at the book.

James, my son, please forgive me. You are the one blessing which has made me hesitate.

CHAPTER 7

1

When Nurse Jackie brought Miss Jones's breakfast she stopped at the foot of the bare bed with the tray in her hands, staring at the mattress as if she had been unable to believe what they had told her. Helen was up and dressed, sitting in her chair, her heart racing against the possibility that Nurse Jackie might use Miss Jones as a pretext to talk about what was uppermost in her mind.

The girl put the breakfast tray on the portable table, wheeled the table across Helen's knees. She kept hold of the edges for a few toll-taking seconds, curiously examining Helen's blank stare.

"You don't know anything about it, do you, pet?" she mused. "You're not with us any more." Suddenly she embraced Helen's head tightly against her chest. "Poor thing," she said affectionately, "you just take it all as it comes, don't you?"

It was hard to imagine Nurse Jackie being privy to Hill House's second purpose. She brought up a chair and sat beside Helen while she ate her breakfast. Unusually hungry and wanting to eat at her normal pace, Helen deplored that refinement of her role wherein she had decreed that Miss Jones ate slowly, and wished the nurse away. But as she nibbled she was warmed, recognizing an obscure instinct in Nurse Jackie to atone for the fact that in the night Miss Jones had been treated as what she was—the fitfully illuminated shell of a human being.

"We *are* doing well this morning, aren't we?"

It was hard to be dainty, to offer her groaning stomach such gradual sops. And there turned out to be no bonus from the unwelcome presence: to Helen's disappointment the girl confined her remarks to the progress of Miss Jones's breakfast.

"Thank you very much . . . nice girl . . ." said Miss Jones, as Nurse Jackie picked up the tray from a doubly unsatisfied Helen.

"Bless you." But the nurse's glance now was vague, her thoughts had moved on to the next task. She went quickly out of the room without looking back.

Helen ate a couple of biscuits from the tin beside her bed which was kept stocked by the family at The Laurels, then went downstairs. Sister Wendy was poised on the arm of Miss Protheroe's chair. Beyond them Bournemouth sparkled in the bright sunshine.

Helen drifted across the room.

"Hello, lovey." Sister Wendy offered a momentary compassionate gaze, then turned back to Miss Protheroe. "She was there all the time, you know, at least we think so. No one saw her wandering and when we answered the bell she was in bed asleep. Slept through it all."

"Mrs. Barker rang the bell?"

"Yes. That's awful, isn't it? Shows she changed her mind.

Must have been the last movement the poor lady was capable of."

"When did she die?"

Miss Protheroe's question was Helen's answer. She felt it fall through her mind like a stone, knew as it fell that it would always lie there, too heavy to be pushed away, likely at any time to be exposed to view.

"About half-past five. It was just too late when they found her."

"What did she—use?"

"A penknife. Her own penknife, she showed it to me the other day. She'd already decided . . ."

Sister Wendy's big blue eyes were troubled. But even one of Mr. Jones's ilk could be affected by a tragedy which lay outside the assignment.

I am convinced that Mrs. Barker's death is what it seemed . . .

But Mrs. Barker's chair was empty, and Helen felt mocked by the bright world beyond the windows. She drifted out of the lounge again, into the kitchen. Mrs. Roberts was emerging from the still-room which contained her fridges, store cupboards and deep freeze. She was looking thoughtful, and when she saw Miss Jones she looked cheerful and beamed, but Helen thought there could have been some fleeting intermediate stage in her eyes which she was unable to define.

"Hello, dearie." Mrs. Roberts gave vent to a puffing breath. She sat heavily down on a chair beside the kitchen table. It creaked beneath her weight. "Well," she said, a sadness now in her smile, "at least you're past getting upset. Perhaps you're lucky."

"I'm lucky," repeated Helen. She helped herself to one of a large plateful of scones. "I just thought I might . . ."

"That's right, dear, help yourself." Mrs. Roberts's voice changed as she turned towards Tracy who was trailing across the kitchen floor. "Where on earth have you been, girl? The sink's full."

Tracy said in a mutter, scraping her feet as she went over to the sink, "I've been cleaning up those dining-tables."

"All right," conceded Mrs. Roberts, "but you'd better stay in here now. I'm going up to see Matron."

"Heard about Mrs. Barker?" Tracy raised her voice against the cascade of the taps.

"I heard. They couldn't save her." Mrs. Roberts looked really upset. Miss Jones sat down in the armchair.

"How she *could* . . ." Tracy lifted her red hands out of the water, stared at her red wrists. "Pick up a knife and cut—*your-self* . . ."

"Miss Jones slept through it."

Tracy whirled round, scattering her soapsuds, to look at Helen. "Blimey, Mrs. Roberts, I'd forgotten she was in that room. Wonder what she'd have done if she'd been awake?" *Don't. Please, don't.* "Perhaps she was. Who's to know?"

"No one, I suppose." Mrs. Roberts turned her penetrating gaze on Helen. "And as she seems the same as usual, no one ever will."

Tracy too was staring interestedly at Helen before shrugging back to the sink. Quickly Helen moistened dry lips.

"All right, then," said Mrs. Roberts, taking her overall off and hanging it on the inner door. "You can start peeling potatoes when you've finished there."

Tracy didn't show a response, unless in the intensified clatter under the grey water. Not wanting further fascinated scrutiny, Helen wavered off in Mrs. Roberts's wake.

At least I know that Mrs. Barker didn't want a second chance.

2

For almost an hour, after lunch, she was asleep. Not entirely against her will, although she struggled at first to resist the tide. She thought she was the last one in the silent room to yield to it, although, of course, it was never possible to know whether Mrs. Wellington slept or kept vigil. At least her eyes were shut, on the last circuit to which Helen pushed herself, along with all the other eyes in the room. Miss Welch mut-

tered as she slept, her face still anxious even with its flaring
lamps unlit. Mr. Thomas still half-smiled, Mrs. Charlesworth's
head lay back against her cushion, her lower jaw dropped
down, and her upper teeth . . .

Helen made her last effort. She turned her head to look at
Mrs. Anthony, and Mrs. Anthony's eyes were shut, her breathing was shallow and regular, her face as benevolent as Mr.
Thomas's. Mrs. Stoddart was snoring slightly, lolled like a rag
doll to the side of her chair. Miss Duncan was the only one
whose expression was different in sleep, all the aggression
gone, the lines drooping.

Someone, reflected Helen sleepily, was only pretending to
sleep, or was disciplined even in unconsciousness. Unless it
was Mr. Weston or Mr. Corlett Mr. Jones was after . . . Or
Mrs. Wayne-Jenkins . . .

Miss Protheroe wasn't asleep after all, her eyes were open
and staring at the tumbling blocks of grey and black cloud,
which were the last thing Helen saw . . .

It was Mrs. Wayne-Jenkins, marching in with a visitor, who
wakened her. Mrs. Wayne-Jenkins strode across the room and
sat down unhesitatingly in Mrs. Barker's chair, impatiently
motioning her niece to fetch up one of the stacking chairs
from near the door.

"Do you think you should, Auntie?" The young woman sat
uncertainly down. "I mean . . . she's only just . . . it might
seem a bit . . ."

"Stuff and nonsense!" declared Mrs. Wayne-Jenkins. "A chair
is a chair, Veronica, and if I don't sit in it someone else will."

Beside this self-deprecating, lip-biting, young woman, Miss
Anthony, coming across the room, seemed a paragon of self-
possession. But the very exaggeration of Miss Wayne-Jenkins's
diffidence, reflected in her runaway chin and protruding teeth,
made her more memorable than Miss Anthony.

Refreshed from her rest, Helen was disappointed that Miss
Duncan had no visitor, it would have been a welcome injec-
tion of amusement to see whose conversation, hers or Mrs.
Wayne-Jenkins's, prevailed. As it was, Miss Duncan gave vent
to several sniffs of annoyance and a number of displeased

glances, none of which were lost on Mrs. Wayne-Jenkins. Helen was sure that Miss Duncan, had she been capable of it, would at an early stage have swept out of the room on a caustic comment. But she stayed in her seat, and remembering the weakness of her getting up and going away, Helen felt a pang of pity for so strong a mind in so feeble a body. It was followed by a sense of her own helplessness, of almost panic proportions. Somewhere in the house was a man or woman whose mind was working as clearly as her own, someone who was being nursed back to health to carry on his or her destructive task. And she still had not the slightest idea who that man or woman might be. The only certainty was that Mrs. Barker's death was one suspect less . . .

Sister Wendy was crossing the room followed by a large amiable-looking young woman Helen now knew to be Mr. Thomas's daughter-in-law.

"Come on now, Mr. Thomas!"

"Hello, Dad!"

They had to go very near, and shout.

"Hello," said Mr. Thomas at last, in pleased surprise. "Is it tea-time?" He started to crane towards the mantelpiece. Outside, raindrops were splashing diagonally on to a side window.

"Not yet," said the daughter-in-law. "Anyway, I'm taking you home today for your tea. I'll get your things and meet you in the hall."

Home for Mr. Thomas might be like The Laurels. What might not be said and done in the few hours before he came grinning back among them?—And by Mrs. Wellington, and Mrs. Charlesworth and Miss Welch et al? There was no one who never had a visitor, never went out. Even Miss Anthony, when the sun shone, sometimes came in a taxi instead of by bus and took her mother for a run by the sea . . . But none of them needed to go out, for goodness' sake.

Mr. Thomas had got only as far across the room as Miss Duncan's chair. Miss Duncan looked up, because of his shadow, then crossly down.

"You're in my light, Mr. Thomas." She said it to her book.

"In your light? That will never do." He took a couple of

steps in the direction of the door. "Is that better? I'm so very
sorry. A good book, is it?" Miss Duncan didn't answer. "I
always like—"

"There's too much noise in here," announced Mrs. Wellington, without opening her eyes.

"Oh God," said Miss Duncan.

"Come along, come along," said Mr. Thomas's daughter-in-
law from the doorway.

"I'm coming." Mr. Thomas now completed his journey
across the room.

"I'd like to have taken you out," said Miss Anthony to her
mother, "but it really didn't look fit. And you see . . ."

The sun had completely disappeared, and rain was splashing on each of the three sides of the window. Helen saw Miss
Protheroe shake her head and take a rare overt glance round
the room.

"Good afternoon to you all."

In the doorway now was Mrs. Stoddart's sister, slender,
beautifully dressed, her fur jacket over her arm. All quality, it
would seem, with her soft Edinburgh voice and warm smile for
everyone as she glided gently past. But then, how Mr. Jones
impressed people, too!

"Shall I make the tea here?" queried Mrs. Stoddart. "Or
would it be nice to go out today?"

"We'll go out, dear. We won't notice the weather in Allen's."

"Not what it was, Allen's," boomed Mrs. Wayne-Jenkins.

Helen decided it was Mrs. Wayne-Jenkins who made the
lounge feel too small. She followed Mrs. Stoddart and her sister
when they left the room and wavered upstairs. Then without
much hope she tried Mrs. Wayne-Jenkins's door. It gave, and
she went into the room, leaving the door ajar behind her.

There was a strong smell of perfumed cosmetic. She shook
free of it and began a systematic search, quickly, with an eye
and ear always for the landing. Mr. Jones's team had given her
lessons in casing a room thoroughly and with speed, and she
tried to put them into practice, buoyed by the knowledge that
Miss Jones's investigations did not always stop short at the surface of things.

There seemed to be nothing, even among the papers, of possibly sinister import.

But would there be, for heaven's sake?

Helen was about to push the last drawer shut, when she noticed a packet of throat lozenges. She picked it up, opened it, and put two of them into her mouth, facing the fact that since she had gone to sleep after lunch she had had a sore throat and a heavy head.

3

The lozenges didn't help her throat. Nor did her tea. During the evening the rawness increased, and she kept wanting to cough. She began to feel relieved that she had to hang on only until the next day. Because she would rather be ill at The Laurels than at Hill House. And because Miss Jones would be as helpless as a kitten in asking for the appropriate first aid.

She gave in to the easy absorption of an old film, which took her up to the hot drink and bedtime. The hot drink seemed to have a disproportionate effect on her body temperature and then, on the stairs with Nurse Jackie, she was shudderingly cold.

She was afraid the nurse would feel it in her trembling arm, but her thoughts were far away and she left Helen almost at the bedroom door. The bedspread was over Mrs. Barker's bed, and Helen for the first time considered the hazard of a new neighbour. But there were no unfamiliar things in the room to replace Mrs. Barker's. The notebook, of course, had gone from the locker, along with all Mrs. Barker's other things. As if she had never been.

In bed, Helen lay shivering. Her throat was getting more and more painful and she was finding it increasingly hard to swallow and to breathe. She didn't set her inner alarm, but woke to moonlight because of being cold and uncomfortable and wanting to go to the lavatory. Helen, hugging herself against the trembling of her body, went along the landing to the bathroom at the head of the stairs. When she came out, she seemed to see two things simultaneously: Nurse Sandra smiling at her from the lighted booth opposite. And a young man just either opening or closing her bedroom door.

She had tightened her mask before she left the bathroom, and it stood her in good stead. As, in a way, did the unfamiliar light-headedness of her physical condition. Slowly, with a half smile, she advanced towards her bedroom, aware that Nurse Sandra was on her feet, must surely be making her leisured, yawning way to the door of the booth. *Not too leisured,* prayed Helen Markham, but a long way off . . .

The young man had frozen, his hand still on the doorknob, watching Miss Jones as she approached him with her imbecile smile and apparent lack of fear. Helen remarked him as she moved slowly forward, his medium height, his slight figure dressed in denims with open-necked shirt, his short crudely cut brown hair, pale face, moustache, cold grey eyes. As she stared his outline seemed to waver, and for an absurd second she thought she knew him . . .

Miss Jones, almost beside the motionless figure, made a groping movement between him and the bedroom door. "Do you think . . ." She looked confidingly into the expressionless face. "Want to go . . . Can I get . . ."

If she couldn't get to lie down she thought she might faint— from weakness rather than from fear. But two more things seemed to happen at the same time: a door clicked loudly behind her, and the young man was gone. Along the corridor which led to the staff kitchen and the frosted window, she was sure of that, but he had gone so silently, so quickly, she would have no memory of his crossing the landing . . .

"Well now, Miss Jones. Out of bed again!"

She let herself rest against the wall as she turned round to Nurse Sandra, standing there smiling indulgently, relaxed, having seen nothing. Having saved Helen from—what? Something she would not—could not—just now think about.

"Want to go to bed . . ."

"Of course you do, you silly girl!" Nurse Sandra pushed the bedroom door open, snapped on the light, took Helen's arm in a firm kind hand. She stood in the doorway as Helen, scarcely acting, wavered towards her bed.

"Good night, Miss Jones!"

The darkness was restored, the door closed. She must sleep before she began to worry. About her health or her safety . . . She slept.

It was broad daylight when she awoke. At first she lay rigid with dismay at how she felt, then went systematically over herself to assess the deterioration. Her limbs ached, the skin of her back and front was tender, her head ached too, as if the young man of the night (if he had been real) had dealt her a blow, her eyeballs were made of cotton wool, someone had shoved soap up her nose. And when she eventually dragged herself to the edge of the bed she needed all her willpower not to flop back on the pillow.

But at least it was Friday, and someone would be there at two o'clock to take her away. Until then, she would just have to rely on the fact that most people hardly ever really looked at Miss Jones.

In the mirror her face was white and shrunken, her eyes enormous. Mercifully, Nurse Jackie seemed in a hurry and dashed off as soon as she had set down the breakfast tray. Helen managed the bread and butter, but squashed the egg through the mesh of the wash basin, followed by the marmalade, because however Mrs. Markham felt Miss Jones would not have lost her appetite. By the time she was ready to go downstairs she was hard put to it to control the shivering, and she went first to the men's bedroom and sat in the chair between Mr. Weston and Mr. Corlett, in direct line with their electric fire. Both pairs of eyes were alert, particularly Mr. Weston's, and she noticed them on her from time to time, but the men talked across her as if she wasn't there. She left them because she was all at once suffocatingly hot, and then she went downstairs holding on to the banister and straight to her chair in the lounge, hoping for a bland lunch.

"Oops-a-daisy! We're a bit wobbly today, aren't we?"

That really must be as far as she allowed any of them to go. On her feet, Helen summoned all her strength to walk

unaided into the dining-room and sit down. She put her hands
up as if to help Nurse Hazel with the bib, and the glands in
her neck were like picture cord. It was roast lamb, and she
made the most of the concealing properties of a large piece of
gristle. Ground rice was manageable, and slightly soothed her
throat. It was fortunate that speech was so subdued a part of
the Miss Jones role. Helen had tested her voice mid-morning
in the cloakroom, and it had been replaced by a croak.

She got back to her place somehow, and sat staring into the
blinds. Everyone but she, Miss Protheroe and Miss Duncan
appeared to be asleep. Miss Anthony arrived, then Miss
Welch's sister. Now there was another strange young man in
the doorway, unless to see strange young men was a symptom
of her illness. This one was not like the young man of the
night. This one was tall and good-looking, smartly dressed,
dark hair well-cut and brushed. He was coming across the
room to her, he was there, bending over her, there was nothing she could do. He was kissing the corner of her mouth . . .

"Wake up, Miss Jones, dear, here's your nephew!"

"I don't . . . I can't . . ."

"You haven't seen him for such a long time, dear. Your
nephew!"

The young man had moved slightly away from her and she
could see him properly. Rupert. Rupert last seen outside the
ladies' dressing-room at the Reddington Rep.

"Hello, Auntie darling."

He took the kiss again now, at the corner of her mouth, as
he had taken it unscripted so often on stage. When he
straightened up he seemed to waver in the aquamarine light
cast by the blinds. But the whole room was wavering. She
didn't know if he was part of another dream into which she
had fallen, but she didn't feel any surprise that he was there.
With her last strength she pulled herself to her feet, pushed
her arm through his, gave him her weight. She was aware of
his face jerking round towards her, and then they were walking to the door. In the hall she staggered as he left her to take
her coat from Sister Wendy, but managed to stay on her feet.
She fumbled into the coat. Luckily they always gave her

plenty of help on the steps. The sparkling air, the sunshine, made her whole body ripple with gooseflesh, then she was in the car, trying not to weep in the relief of it, not making any more effort.

Rupert was beside her, the car was moving, they were on their way.

"Thorough as ever, I see," murmured Rupert, his eyes on the road.

"That was Helen Markham," she whispered. "You see, I've got 'flu and I'm dying."

CHAPTER 8

1

The small pebbles at the edge of the tide moved as the water moved over them. It wasn't much of a tide, just a very slight regular movement, dragging to and fro. It didn't bother her, what bothered her were the words which kept travelling across the pebbles. The man at my door. The man at my door. Was someone playing Ravel's *Bolero*, or was the sound of it in her head? So hot . . . As soon as the words had crossed over they reappeared on the left and crossed over again. If she could only remember what came next she was sure the whole procession would finally pass by and leave her in peace. But she couldn't remember . . .

I must write my report. I must write my report.

She didn't know when the words changed but she had been half-listening to the anxious voice for some time before she realized it was her own. Cora was sitting beside the bed, wiping her forehead with a deliciously cool damp cloth. She looked relaxed.

"Tomorrow, perhaps," said Cora. "We're not worrying."

Helen knew they were not. Even under the delirium—how long had it lasted, hours or days?—she had known. That they realized she hadn't chosen to be ill.

"I'm all right now," she said drowsily to Cora, stretching her legs, all at once perfectly comfortable. The pebbles were no longer moving, they were the pattern on the curtains, and if she tried she could recall what was worrying her. Only she needn't bother trying just yet.

"You will be," said Cora. "Just go to sleep."

Cora went out of the room and Helen lay contented. She knew already that the contentment wouldn't last, but while it was there she savoured it.

She reviewed the things she was beginning to remember.

Rupert had said in the car, "I always fancied you, you know."

And when she hadn't responded, he had said; "If you'd fancied me, we would have learned more about you. But at least we learned how unsuggestible you are."

It was only now that she realized this was interesting. At the time she had said, "I'm not suggestible to unsolicited onslaught," and had giggled, as if she was drunk and rather pleased to have got her tongue round a difficult phrase.

"I had my orders."

"I don't doubt it." That was the moment she had realized how terribly ill she felt.

He had almost had to carry her into The Laurels. It had been like delirium then, being carried by Rupert again as a mindless creature, but into a house instead of across a stage.

When he said to Cora in the hall, "She says she's ill," it roused her for the last time, she told them they ought to be able to see it for themselves, and then fell on the stairs. After that, memory was intermittent, cutting from one short scene to another. Lying on the bed, being covered up and expecting to be comfortable and not being. Hearing voices, advancing and retreating like the curtain pebbles, and feeling a sudden heavy dull pain in her arm. Her body surface no longer had that strange numb feeling to it. Nor was her throat sore, although her chest was when she breathed too deeply. Carefully she turned over on to her side, and could rest.

She turned back to find Mr. Jones standing by the bed. She knew she had been deeply asleep.

"How are you?" He was searching her face.

"I'm fine. I thought I was all right when Cora was here. But I'm much better now. Have you been here before?"

"Yes."

The contentment was already beginning to disintegrate.

"I'm sorry."

"Don't be silly."

"They say that if you're really dedicated you can keep illness at bay. Flop after you've finished. I hadn't finished. I hadn't really begun."

"That's silly too."

"I don't think it's silly."

She was crying. Then coughing, which hurt her chest.

"How long have I been ill?"

"Four days. It's Tuesday night."

"I should have gone back yesterday!"

"A week won't hurt."

"What on earth's been the matter?"

"Pneumonia. Just. But the doctor says you're run down."

"That's nonsense." She moved her head impatiently on the pillow. "I didn't let them know, you know, that I was ill."

"I know you didn't. If you feel up to it tomorrow, you can start to dictate your report into my machine."

She said drowsily, "I do have one or two things to tell you. Like the young man on the landing."

She wasn't looking at him, but she felt his jerk to attention.

"Young man on the landing?"

The business normality of his voice made her realize how unaccustomedly gentle he had just been.

"Thursday night. I'd been to the loo, the one at the top of the stairs. When I came out I saw that the nurse in the night staff place had spotted me, and I also saw a young man with his hand on the knob of my bedroom door."

"Going in or coming out?"

"No way of knowing."

"And you . . . ?"

"I saw the nurse get to her feet and I just went towards the man and did a bit of Miss Jones' silly business and then the nurses' door clicked open and he'd gone."

"Gone where?"

"Down the corridor where the staff rooms are. There's a window at the end. I'm afraid I don't know whether or not anyone caught him, I went to sleep right away when I was back in bed and I don't think I would have heard anything."

"You don't have to be afraid. I mean . . . You did very well. You're sure . . . ?"

"Absolutely sure." Fear had crept in through the only crack which at present was open to it, because she could tell Mr. Jones was more worried than he was letting her see.

"So you went back to bed. The nurse hadn't noticed anything amiss?"

"Oh no. She just propelled me into the bedroom and waited at the door while I got into bed. I only just made it." The crack that had let in the fear widened slightly. She tried to laugh. "And I've only just realized that the nurse might not, after all, have been my salvation."

Mr. Jones stared at her for a moment, before his next question. "What was the young man like?"

She told him. Mr. Jones continued to pace the room. After a moment he turned abruptly and came back to the bed.

"Look, you must go to sleep now, you really mustn't talk any more tonight. I was to tell you there's a hot drink coming."

She turned her head and saw the covered plate on the bedside table.

"What's that?"

"Something Mrs. Gray said you should eat." He went round the bed to investigate. He was wearing a blue polo-necked jersey and looked his younger self. The plate contained three pieces of thin bread and butter. "If you can," he said.

Mrs. Gray came in with a cup and saucer. Steam rose from the cup.

"You haven't eaten your bread and butter," she said sternly.

"My fault. Good night." Mr. Jones left the room.

Sitting up against the pillows comfortably rearranged by Mrs. Gray, Helen ate the bread and butter and drank the hot milk. Then, before she had time to start thinking, she slept.

2

She awoke to broad daylight and Mrs. Gray drawing back the curtains. She could eat toast now as well as drink tea, and read the paper. It was slightly reassuring to be reminded there was a world beyond her own. After an hour or so she made it almost sure-footed to the bathroom and back again. Cora was in the bedroom and helped her back in bed.

"Thanks. Mr. Jones said I could dictate my report."

"I'll see to it. How do you feel?" asked Cora with interest.

"Clear in the head at least. I don't like to think how weak I am. I want to get on with the job."

"Only when you're fit, or you'll cause more trouble than you're worth. When did you realize you were ill?" Despite the time of day Cora was clearly her afternoon self.

"After lunch on Thursday. It was just a sore throat and a headache at first. But it made me want to cough."

"It must have been a bit creepy. You found a young man, we hear." In her sudden attentiveness Cora made her think of Mr. Jones.

"No one and nothing else, though. Except . . ."

Cora was leaning over her. "What is it?"

It was awful but it was only now that she remembered Mrs. Barker. At The Laurels they might not even know of it. But for the moment she wasn't worrying about that. She lay with closed eyes, unable to speak without weeping.

"We know what happened to Mrs. Barker," came Cora's voice softly. "They told us when we rang to say we were keeping you at home until you're better. And we don't imagine you really slept through that night."

"No." She kept her eyes shut, although it meant she was looking at the moonlit bedroom at Hill House. "I rang the bell. They thought it was her."

"*You* rang the bell?"

"When I saw what she'd done? Of course I did!" She opened her eyes to glare at Cora, but Cora was looking unusually gentle and reflective. "That was the one thing I could do, thank God," said Helen, "which didn't put me in trouble. As it was, I lay there while she bled."

"You could do this sort of work for a lifetime," said Cora, "and not have to make that sort of choice."

"And it's not even really my table, as the waitress said." She heard the hysteria in her laugh.

"Rest again now," said Cora as she got to her feet, "and I'll bring the machine up later."

"I'd like it now." Now she was afraid of rest. Making her report could help control the more shocking of her memories. She had also remembered the two sisters at Hill House.

Cora shrugged. "As you wish."

Cora left the room and came straight back with the recorder. She fixed it up and explained it.

"I'm bound to make a false start. Will you leave me to it?"

"Of course." Cora hesitated in the doorway, came back to the bed. "I'm sorry, Helen."

Cora went out and closed the door. Was she really sorry? One thing they had taught her, already, was to suspect anything which didn't have an obvious professional end, which was to suspect gentleness, and regret. It was a lesson which would be hard to unlearn, when her assignment was over.

When her assignment was over?

That, now, was the most unimaginable situation of all.

3

By the time she had apologized into the machine for her embarrassment she was over it and was speaking fluently. As she had hoped, the exercise helped her to subdue her thoughts of Mrs. Barker, her regret at what her own role had been, the ethical conflict of that night at Hill House . . .

The sky was changing as she watched it. When Miss Protheroe looked at the sky, hour after hour, did she see it? Or was she working things out? Could Miss Welch deliberately maintain a permanent expression of terror? It was hard to believe the Miss Welch character would have been chosen as a disguise. So she was inclined to eliminate Miss Welch . . . But nobody else, except that it was so difficult to imagine that anyone as gentle as Mrs. Anthony, as perpetually catatonic as Mrs. Charlesworth, as frail-footed as Miss Duncan and Mrs. Wellington, despite their brains . . . Mr. Thomas smiling his way out to the cloakroom . . . What if a real clue was being displayed before Miss Jones's vacant chair?

Helen realized to her astonishment that she was impatient to get back to Hill House. The astonishment was for the discovery of how little she really knew herself. If she had had advance knowledge of what her assignment would entail, she would have sought the deepest hole to hide herself away from it. And now—strain, danger, fear of death—she was enjoying it. Oh, she would shrink and sweat when the time came to go back, subdue an impulse when she got out of the car to run for her life instead of wavering into Hill House, but she would be ready to carry on.

Her astonishment grew as she thought about her old life, and John. She hadn't thought of John at all for days on end. And now that she was thinking of him, nothing happened, it was as if she was recalling someone else's despair. It didn't seem any less of a sad story, but it concerned some other woman.

Her only personal concern now was what they would do if time went on and she didn't get anywhere. If—

Her only personal concern? Helen stretched her legs in the bed, moved her hands across her hard flat stomach. Somewhere there was a warm area, the idea of something strange . . .

She was startled by the knock at the door. Remembering the log in the grate at the White Swan in Reddington, she wondered if she was more scared of small things than of large. At least awareness of the imminent large brought a helpful flow of adrenalin.

The door opened before she called out. Rupert was in the room, dressed in pale trousers and a check shirt as she remembered him from the theatre, carrying a beaker on a saucer. He came over and put them between her hands.

"Bovril," he said. "How are you?"

"You wouldn't know me!"

"Oh, I think I would." He sat down on the chair by the bed. Looking at him, it surprised her that she had never had a moment's temptation to respond to him, he was attractive in a way she admired. Perhaps it was that she had always been repelled by his assumption of success. He was staring at her.

"Well?" she challenged, over the rim of the beaker.

"Aggressive to the last."

"You talk as if I'd finished. I've barely begun."

"And she talks bravely! Confident, are you?"

"Not as you understand it. But I have to be."

His expression softened. She had always thought he looked less attractive the rare times this happened. Now she saw something in his face she had never seen in Reddington. It looked like a blend of curiosity and concern.

"Of course you do. I know something about the time you've had. I was talking to your trouper instincts."

"Which I appreciate. Are you really a trouper, Rupert?"

"I'm a number of things," he said easily.

"I haven't got anywhere," she said, still with the instinct to forestall him. "My only achievement to date is not being found out."

"You're too modest. You've established a place for yourself where none of us can go. Privileged access."

"If I can only take advantage of it!"

"You will, you will. The thing now is to get better so as to get back. And to do that you should relax while you can."

"I know, I suppose."

"Then do it. Is there any reading matter you particularly fancy?"

She had to think a few moments to remember Helen Markham's tastes, the books she had chosen to read each night, in bed beside her sleeping husband. And later alone at Mrs. Molyneux's.

"Bring me some thick Victorian novels."

"Will do." Rupert got up, stared at her for a moment (still, she thought, curious), then turned and went out of the room. She found she had expected a flirtatious phase to his visit, and was surprised that it had not come. But, as with Cora, there was a new element in his manner, as if all at once she counted. Some instinct told her it had to do with more than the fact that she was ill. It made her uneasy . . .

There might have been something in the Bovril, because the next event was her lunch tray, and she was able to rouse herself only for the five or ten minutes needed to eat most of it. When she woke up properly she knew that hours had gone by. The window was covered in rain and Mr. Jones was again standing by the bed. He looked grave, but then more often than not he did.

"Hello," she said sleepily.

"Hello." He indicated the chair. "May I?"

"Of course." She was surprised he had asked. Slowly he sat down and for a moment they were both silent. She turned her head on the pillow and looked at the soft outlines of his profile. Unusually, his hair had fallen over his forehead, making him look young even though he was formally dressed.

"I've read your report. I'm sorry about Mrs. Barker."

"Thank you."

"In this job," he said softly, "one thinks the hardest experience is behind, and then there comes something worse. If it's any consolation, I think you did just right."

"Helen Markham no longer feels she's doing anything."

His gaze intensified.

"So long as she's never tempted to look for glory."

"I hope I'm not such a fool." She spoke with dignity, then on a pang of fear. "Remember I'm only a temp. You must leave me capable of running my own life when this is over."

Even as she said it, she wondered what that was. He turned to look at her again.

"You mean the Reddington Repertory Company?"

His voice and his face were without expression.

"I mean living without danger and deceit. And fear of pain and death." She heard the defiance in her voice. But she wasn't really protesting about the job, she was trying to make a point at Mr. Jones. Perhaps he had been right to warn her against her ego.

"None of us lives without those things," he said, "if you think about it." He got to his feet. "Mrs. Gray will be coming now with a hot drink, and then you must sleep until morning. Perhaps tomorrow you can get up."

He left the room without looking at her again.

CHAPTER 9

1

Helen's convalescence was rapid and should have been more enjoyable than it was. But behind the relaxation and the reading, the tempting food and the stimulus of conversation, there ran a thread of anxiety. Again and again she tried to pin it to the hard-etched memory of the young man at her door in Hill House, but always it twitched away . . .

"I feel like a capon being fattened for the oven."

She said it on Friday morning to Rupert, when she had moved down to the small conservatory, and he brought her a cup of coffee. Watching him, she saw the jerk of his head towards her and his widening eyes. The thread tightened.

And she had almost meant what she had said. They were all so solicitous towards her, Cora permanently her after-lunch self, chatting, playing Scrabble, Rupert being attentive without being flirtatious or too jokey, even Mrs. Gray breaking her dourness with the odd kindly remark.

But in this world where every action had a practical meaning, such concern could scarcely be for her *beaux yeux*.

So, for what?

Only Mr. Jones, although not these days severe, seemed remote and serious and not much in evidence except for business.

Before lunch on Friday he called her into the office and she supplemented her report, dredging up every nuance of behaviour which she had observed at Hill House, and which she found was now floating with renewed clarity to the surface of her mind. Not that it amounted to much. The only possible discovery was the young man on the landing.

"I must ask you again, now you're better. You're certain you were Miss Jones?"

"I'm certain—aided no doubt by my genuine deterioration." The submerged fear made her go on. "He could just be a boyfriend of one of the nurses, couldn't he? We don't know—"

"No, we don't know." All at once there was a black line on the pristine blotter.

"I want to get back, Mr. Jones."

They stared at one another and then Mr. Jones rose abruptly to his feet and went over to the window, where he stood with his face close to the curtain. "Next week. If you continue to improve over the weekend."

"Oh, I will." She felt suddenly out of breath. "It was strange," she said, half in order to say something, "but my first reaction when I saw the man was that I knew him."

"What!"

She had all his trained attention.

"No . . . I'm afraid I can't think it means anything. And the feeling had gone almost as soon as it came. Anyway . . ." She was still trying to talk her breathlessness away. "I was pretty light-headed."

"It's an odd reaction to have without foundation. Work on it." Mr. Jones came back from the window and sat down. "Try to take it unawares. Go and rest now before lunch, close your eyes and recreate the moment when you saw the man. It might give you something, and anyway I think you should rest."

She felt the tweak of anxiety. Now even Mr. Jones was

showing this extraordinary concern for her. But that was absurd, he simply wanted an entirely fit operator . . .

Logical explanation, or illogical fear, she didn't like the taste of either.

"I'm all right," she said aggressively. "I'm quite better."

"Almost." He was still watching her, and for the first time it was to the point of embarrassment. "You must build up your strength."

She got up. "You really don't have to keep saying that."

She wanted an edge to their exchanges, to cut through the concern which was beginning to feel more restrictive than her actual confinement at The Laurels.

But Mr. Jones merely said mildly, "It's in the interests of all of us."

She had to restrain herself not to bang the door behind her. But for a moment there was a relief in feeling aggrieved.

After lunch she was sent with Cora into the garden. It was out there, paradoxically, that she felt again the claustrophobia which made her want to run and run. As it was, she sought and obtained Cora's permission to gallop up and down the confined permitted length, and was glad to find herself so quickly exhausted.

"But you are feeling really better, aren't you?" urged Cora, as she sat slowly down on the seat where Helen had collapsed breathless.

"Yes, oh yes. I just get tired rather quickly after being so lazy. And I don't need that sort of energy, do I? I'll probably play Miss Jones better than ever to next week's houses. I shall be completely restored by Monday," she added hastily, remembering she was still a junior employee of a ruthless organization despite so much seeming evidence to the contrary, and that jokes about work were hardly in order. And she thought she had seen the old familiar coldness threaten in Cora's eyes. But Cora said dreamily now, relaxing her head against the back of the seat,

"That's good."

"Is there anything you want me to do before I go back?"

The way Cora jerked upright and stared at her reminded

Helen of Rupert's reaction that morning. What had she said to Rupert which had seemed to startle him? She couldn't remember. But maybe she had imagined a reaction from Cora, who was leaning back again and gazing at the hard blue sky.

"Anything we want you to do?" she murmured.

"I mean, aren't we going to do any revision, take any sort of refresher course?"

Cora laughed, with uncharacteristic heartiness.

"That's hardly necessary. You're a professional, you'll think yourself back into your role."

It was another paradox of this small closed world, that its protagonists were so sensitively aware of strengths and weaknesses and reactions, without seeming to be aware of, and certainly not interested in, the person they added up to. But of course the lesson they had learned, the lesson Helen was also learning despite herself, was to disregard anything which was not strictly necessary for their business purpose.

2

After the garden, Cora suggested Helen might like to go back into the conservatory, and it was there that Rupert brought her *Middlemarch*.

He sat down beside her, brushing aside her thanks. Even when she asked him if he knew how Jonathan was there was no suspicion of knowingness.

"He was all right when I last saw him, but that wasn't very recently."

"Are you still with the company?"

"No. You'll remember, I was temporary too. Had a sudden impulse to exercise that side of my many-faceted character, and was lucky, small repertory companies always being so short of handsome young men who can also act."

He grinned at her and she grinned back.

"Of course, of course. But I'm sorry you've no news of Jonathan. It's hard for me to imagine by now that he or the company exists."

Rupert looked sympathetic, giving another twist to her disquiet.

"It's the nature of this particular assignment. In a way, though, it makes life simpler when one gets a closed assignment, one isn't having to perpetrate small deceptions all the time, tell perpetual little lies."

"Well, that's something I shan't be able to compare. Seeing that I'm engaged for the one job only."

"Of course."

She was uncomfortably aware that he had looked away from her.

But when he had gone she stretched her legs in the long chair and realized she was well again, with a sense of urgency about her role which would soon make her restless.

And John had been wont to say, "I don't know what the Lady Helen would do without her Lord."

She had not been able to restrain herself from throwing the remark at him when he told her he was leaving. He had turned away, she saw him turning away in her head as she lay back in the reclining chair in the conservatory at The Laurels, but although the scene was vivid it was between two people she didn't know very well . . .

"Tea is in the drawing-room."

The sudden coolness across her body was Mrs. Gray, standing between her and the sun.

Rupert and Cora were in the drawing-room already, and Cora was pouring tea. They were in a cheerful mood which at moments seemed to Helen to possess a feverish edge. But she had so schooled herself to look for significance she was probably being over-imaginative. At any rate, she laughed too. As they began eventually to stack the crockery back on the trolley, she asked if either or both of them would like a game of Scrabble.

Rupert and Cora glanced quickly at each other, the concerted glances which always re-alerted Helen to the real situation.

"Don't you think it would be a better idea for you to have a lie-down before dinner?" asked Cora. Helen wasn't deceived. The order was that she must rest.

For what ordeal?

"Oh, all right, perhaps I could do with it."

There was an unstated procedure of maintaining an illusion of choice at those points where the brief obtruded.

"The wind was tiring today," observed Cora, "even for those who aren't convalescent."

"Yes." They watched her as she trailed out of the room. Upstairs, briefly, anger took over again, but really, uneasiness was the sensation she was living with. She lay down on the bed, staring across the room at the featureless sky, forcing herself to rethink the moment when the young man had been near enough for her to see his features and she had thought . . . No, she hadn't thought anything, she had felt . . . The expression in the eyes, or lack of it? The poise of the head?

There was a tap on the door, and Cora put her head round.

"Oh, Helen," she said, "we forgot to mention there's a bit of a dinner-party tonight. Will you wear your black? It's your most elegant."

"All right." The oversight was surprising, but she did feel best in her black dress. "What are you going to wear?"

Uncharacteristically Cora hesitated. "I shan't be here. But I'll see you tomorrow. Be down at half past seven, by the way, if you will."

She closed the door and Helen lay down again, fighting a sense of desolation which eventually gave way to curiosity, then to a long appraisal in the glass of her unfamiliar face.

3

When she went into the drawing-room there was only Mr. Jones, looking distinguished in a white jacket and occupied at the drinks cupboard. As he turned round to her she was aware more keenly than ever of how impossible it was, even in this new rigorous world, not to experience the normal unprofessional reaction to a setting, a style of dress, a time of day.

And the normal reaction now, of course, was for Mr. Jones to advance to meet her, for them both to smile in mutual cool approval.

"You look lovely," he said lightly, abnormally.

"Thank you," she said lightly, amazed.

She saw the champagne bottle on the side table. He handed her a glass.

"I'm glad you can accept a compliment, Mrs. Markham. So many Englishwomen turn a compliment aside."

She realized for the first time how often she had tried to imagine him in a purely social situation. Not that she could be sure, of course, that even now he considered himself to be in one. His eyes, as always since the evening they had met in Reddington, were engaging hers all the time he spoke to her, but now she could not help but see that they held admiration. Some vague feeling which had been with her for what seemed a long time began tentatively to identify itself. And an exhilaration, which she recognized at once.

"The only compliments I've received in a long while," she said, smiling, "were Rupert's in Reddington when he was under orders. They didn't, to my good fortune, do very much for me."

"And mine?"

It was extraordinary, how it needed only two insignificant words for her to begin to understand, with entrancing slow recognition, what the vague feeling had been. Her exhilaration surged.

"I have been old and ugly," she said, walking past him and going so close to the curtain she could see out into the garden. "Your compliment seals my renaissance." If he was touching her she could not have been more sharply aware that he had followed her and was standing near.

"Who have you invited to dinner tonight?"

She turned slowly and almost reluctantly round, having to force herself to meet his penetrating gaze.

"You will see. Meanwhile a little more champagne. Champagne is good when one has been ill."

He refilled her glass, then his own.

"Your health, Mrs. Markham, your good health."

"And yours, Mr. Jones." She touched her glass to his.

"I was going to say to you," murmured Mr. Jones, always looking her in the eyes, "that tonight we shall talk no business. But I believe you wouldn't have attempted to do so. You have a sense of fitness."

"I take that as a second compliment. The world can be divided into those who have, and those who haven't. At least, as far as one's own ideas are concerned."

"A sense of fitness is always as far as one's own ideas are concerned. To share it with someone else is a rare and valuable thing."

"I know."

"You shared it with your husband?"

It was like picking up a book on a subject she had once studied closely, been examined in, and then let drop.

"I don't know. I must have thought so. But of course not at the end."

"Are you still very unhappy, Helen?"

She stood stock-still, absorbing his use of her name. She said softly, "I don't think about it any more. When John left me, I thought I was."

"And now?"

"Now? This week? This minute?" She could feel the brilliance of her smile.

"Of course, I should like best to know whether you are unhappy this minute."

"No." The monosyllable was like a confession and fell into too heady a silence. Quickly she broke it. "But I should have thought happiness and unhappiness were irrelevant concepts. Dangerous, even."

"When one has learned the disciplines, one can allow happiness within limits."

"Happiness within limits? I thought happiness was something which came unawares, like angels."

"Of course it can do that. But some of the best operators I've known have been what I'd call happy people. They worked well because they had a sort of lining which kept them calm."

"Don't you mean contentment? Happiness, for goodness' sake, has a bit more blood!"

He said, after a pause, "Yes, it has," and there was something in his voice which made her imagination loop and soar.

Mr. Jones was saying that they should go in to dinner. She had never felt so light on her feet. She tried to fix the sensation in her memory, so that she could recall it when she sank into a chair at Hill House.

She found herself hesitating outside the dining-room door, turning back to look at him, and he put his hand on her elbow and urged her ahead.

She stopped again in the doorway. The curtains had been drawn against the dusk and candles lit on the table, flickering over flowers. Two places had been laid. In silence he walked past her into the room and pulled out the chair at the foot of the table, opposite his.

It was easy to react as coolly as he was reacting, to conceal until later—oh yes, she knew it all, already—her response. She must have learned some prudence from her experience with John, not to have recognized her desire until she had found out it was to be granted. And it had been growing unobserved, because it was already immune to any revelation which might await her of the how and why. She already knew it would be granted with the knowledge of everyone who used The Laurels, even that Mr. Jones could be merely the operative member of a team.

He gave her a little more champagne.

Mrs. Gray came in, and served a soufflé. Mr. Jones went on talking while she was in the room.

"How would you like me to entertain you?"

"Tell me as much as you're at liberty to about yourself. Probably that's the part I shall find the most interesting, anyway."

"The small things which make youthful autobiographies so fascinating. We compare them, of course, with our own early memories. Well, I ran away from school."

"You surprise me right away. Homesickness, or dislike of being institutionalized?"

He gave her one of his doubly attentive looks, no longer veiling admiration.

"My mother thought I was homesick. Perhaps I was, I was fond of her. But I missed my private room."

There were moments when she was almost blinking against the dazzle of possibilities. Most of all against the bright light of certainty. But perhaps the moment now, the moment Mr. Jones had drawn her attention to, was the best one, like all moments of joyous anticipation.

"I didn't like boarding-school either. But you know all about me."

"I know all the facts of you." They stared in silence. He said at last, softly, "And I think I may know you, too."

As they stared they leaned slightly towards one another, across the oval shine of the table, and then he got up and touched the bell, preserving the fragile shimmer in which they floated and which, once other stages had been reached, was a paradise not to be regained.

Mrs. Gray brought in salmon. Helen regretted not being more hungry.

"How did you get into—the work you're in now?"

"Chance."

She felt that, for the first time since they had met, he was doing no more than appeared on the surface—talking and listening in a situation where he was content to be.

"No burning convictions?"

"Convictions, yes. Probably best not to burn too brightly." He grinned at her. The turn of her heart explained, now, her earlier reactions when he had done this.

"No, I suppose you wouldn't burn." She herself was on fire with excitement but the only sign of it she gave was to look candidly, now, into his eyes. She didn't want to dictate his pace, merely to offer reassurance.

"Nor you," he said.

"I don't know what I do, any more."

"You've changed?"

"Or found out things about myself. I astonish myself."

"And you astonish me. Daily. Hourly." The sudden unfamiliar twist to his mouth, as if something had briefly hurt him, made her look delightedly away. He got up and rang the bell. Mrs. Gray brought in fruit and cheese, cleared the rest of the meal. This time they sat in silence while she was in the room.

He looked moody, eating a pear in grave-faced silence. When he had pushed his plate away he got up to pour the last of the champagne. Standing beside her he put his hand on her shoulder, more gently than he had placed it there in the past. The spot throbbed like a wound.

"I should like it," he said, "for this now to be your regular seat at table." He leaned down and kissed her lightly on the mouth. The prospect of mutual generosity was too bright to think about. She still withheld her response.

"And how will Cora like it?"

Cora always sat opposite her father.

"Ah yes." He walked away from her, sat down. Anything to do with Cora was a tricky subject for him, now. "You are, I suppose, being very sophisticated."

"Cora and Rupert," she said, "have these last few days treated me like a piece of fragile china destined intact for a royal table."

"You had no theories as to why?"

"None. It's bothered me."

"That I'm sorry about. And now?"

She smiled at him, confident as yet of her self-control.

"Now, I know you've announced a new policy to Cora and Rupert. In regard to me."

He wasn't disconcerted. "I've told them—what I hope for. There can be nothing—of this kind—hidden in our world. In that sense I made an announcement."

"What you hope for. Or is hoped. Presumably you are part of a hierarchy. Is it—another order?"

Something, so far as the candlelight would let her see, let her distinguish between the internal and external shadows, had quivered in his face.

"Actually no." His voice was quiet and cold.

"But you see it, yourself, as an advanced part of my training. And Rupert having failed."

It was the worst thing she was going to say, but it was the worst thing she could say, and for a moment she was aghast. It wasn't even (unknown woman that she had become) as if she was disturbed by the prospect that she might be stating the truth; but Mr. Jones must be made to see that she was accepting no more than she was being offered.

He had sat back in his chair and was staring at her, but in his old way, entirely without expression. She felt herself shiver, the glorious certainty wavered with the candlelight, but she couldn't retract. She mustn't retract, even though she wanted to tell him it didn't matter, nothing mattered except that, for whatever reason, a new prospect lay between them, moving together towards moments when neither of them could pretend any more . . . If he sent her away now, she would die of desolation.

"You cannot," she said very quietly, "in any sort of fairness object to what I've said." She recognized the moment to correct and explain in a word. "Julian."

He looked at her as he had looked in the past when she had said or done something to make him take notice. He got up with no further reaction and rang the bell. "We'll have coffee and brandy in the drawing-room."

He walked behind her across the hall, not touching her. In the drawing-room, she sat down in a corner of the settee. To her infinite solace, when he had poured the brandies he came and sat beside her. Mrs. Gray put the coffee tray in front of Helen.

"Thank you, Mrs. Gray." Watching his profile as he smiled up at Mrs. Gray, Helen saw he was unnaturally pale. If she had not grown so cautious now, since John, she would think that he was moved, that what he was now devising for her was different in essence from his earlier schemes, not merely in degree. "Go to bed any time you like, Mrs. Gray," said Mr. Jones. "We'll tidy up here."

"Thank you. Good night." Mrs. Gray smiled at Helen as well, went out and closed the door. Helen poured coffee.

Slowly she turned to him, in time to see that his glass was

trembling in his hand. He set it down. He was not so pale as she had thought. There was a flush on his cheekbones.

Her rush of feeling was so strong she had to clench her hands together in her lap, then brush aside a memory of Miss Jones. She smiled at him, less guardedly than she had ever smiled at him before.

"It's only now that I know how and why I've done what I've done at Hill House." She dropped her eyes, but still smiled.

"Why?"

"Because I haven't wanted to fail in any task you set me."

She looked up, and they stared at one another. She had never known anything so clearly and uncomplicatedly and completely. It was the most exhilarating moment of her life, and in it she remembered how she had told John to slow down, that she wasn't ready to commit herself.

She felt herself starting to grin again at the marvellous contrast in the memory. She was so happy it was easy to go on appearing to be independent.

She didn't know the room he led her to, through the silent house. And he didn't know what she was really telling him in her response to him through the night. When she slept she dreamed of rooms, lofty and beautiful, leading into other rooms and out to gardens and distant countryside. There were always more rooms, and although she wanted each time to go back to the one she had just passed through, she was quickly enchanted by the next one. When Julian left her the sun was up and the birds were singing in the garden at The Laurels, and after she had slept again Mrs. Gray deposited the breakfast tray, drew the curtains and said her good-mornings, precisely as she had done these things hitherto across the landing.

CHAPTER 10

1

"It's incest, Mr. Jones!"

"Yes, Miss Jones. The authorities would indeed be interested. And the unauthorized would be interested too. You're trapped."

When the whispering stopped there were drowsy bird-sounds. There was a grey-white crack of light where the curtains met.

She took his travelling finger between her lips. "Did you still feel today you were getting special treatment?"

"No more special. Less, perhaps, except that Cora . . ."

"Yes?"

"Cora told me I looked beautiful."

"Cora said that?"

"I can't see whether or not you look surprised."

"Feel for it." He put her hand on his cheek. The dimple was deeply etched beside his smiling mouth.

"What announcement did you make? A puff of white smoke?"

"I merely ordered breakfast for you in here. There must still be an hour or two before your second breakfast . . . Come here . . . What is it, my love, your face is wet?"

"It's Mrs. Barker. I just suddenly felt that last look of hers. Just felt it now. She so wretched, and I so . . ."

"Wretched?"

"No. Oh no. I think that's why I'm crying. That anyone could be so wretched and still leave someone else able to be so happy." She was sobbing, almost painfully, in his arms. "I might have been able to give her some comfort and I didn't and she disappeared. For ever and without trace."

"There's a trace of her left in you, I should say."

"I hope so."

"Don't think of it too precisely now."

"Oh, I shan't." She moved against him. "I think that's why I was crying."

2

After breakfast on Saturday she had found her way back, to her old room, but Mrs. Gray had taken her aside after lunch and said she would be pleased if Mrs. Markham would accompany her upstairs to see if her belongings had been moved to her satisfaction. Helen followed Mrs. Gray into the room where Julian had led her the night before, to find that everything she had brought with her to The Laurels (which was everything she possessed apart from the few pieces of furniture and the two cases in store) was now disposed in this spacious apartment. It was still her room: there were no evidences of Julian, and it was only after she was in bed that he joined her on those two nights that remained to her, leaving before Mrs. Gray brought in her breakfast.

Downstairs the only overt change was Helen's chair at the dining-table, but the whole flavour of life was different, in a way it took her almost twenty-four hours to define, but which she eventually discovered to be simply that she was no longer subject to the authority of anyone but Julian. And if Julian wasn't there, Cora prefaced any suggestions she had to make with the words "Father asked me to ask you," and Rupert said, "Uncle would like it if." She had the feeling that Cora and Rupert, while approving of developments (unofficially as well as officially), had now become less interested in her. Perhaps they had been interested in the possibility of opposition. Or perhaps it was merely that, having found an identity within the group, she was less conspicuous. Certainly she now felt almost at ease.

It was really her own choice to spend most of the morning alone in her room remembering Miss Jones. Even when she lay resting after lunch (as Julian insisted), she forced herself, with a creditable percentage of success, to think about the young man on the landing at Hill House and her continuing plan of campaign, rather than the nights past and to come— and the uncomfortable longing for Julian to be lying beside her in the daytime as well. She even assumed Miss Jones's face and manner of moving.

Only when she began to get ready for dinner, she allowed herself to be entirely, eagerly, happy.

They were all present for dinner on Sunday night, the night before her return to Hill House. Absurdly at such a moment, poised between an unguaranteed bliss and the possibility of death, she felt for the first time since John had left her that she belonged somewhere, that she had a background to relax against when the pleasure and the pain were over. She had to remind herself, and dutifully did so with little effect, that her situation was as evanescent as it had ever been or could ever be, as evanescent as life on board ship, which breaks up in that moment the side of the ship grates against the quay. The quay for Helen was her return to danger on the morrow, and she could not assume that the ship would sail again.

"Either I am a very good teacher," he said, when they at last lay in bed, "or I merely tapped reserves."

"Yes?"

"You really are so reassuringly contained. Not wasting energy in expressing your tension. I wouldn't know you were turning a hair if I didn't . . ." He took a strand between his fingers, gently pulled it.

"If you didn't . . . ?"

"Begin to know you a little."

"And what does knowing me a little tell you?"

"It tells me you're coiled down and round inside yourself, preparing for your spring. I feel it in your arms, in your wrists and thighs. In the fraction of delay with which your smile has appeared since dinner. In the way your moods have been a little too emphatic today—gravity, gaiety, calm. These are the traces of your tension which is your getting ready and your clamp down on your fear."

"Of course," she whispered, "I am afraid."

He laced her fingers, carried her hand up to his face. "I must tell you something."

"Tell me, then." In spite of her happiness, she knew it was not something good.

"The young man on the landing. He may come again."

"I know." She had known, but until this moment she had managed not to face her knowledge. "To make sure Miss Jones is what she seems."

"I can't make you go back."

It was the most he could say. "I shall go back."

She didn't tell him of the other fear: that from having nothing she now had everything to leave behind. It was impossible to put into words, anyway, without using the phrase she was scrupulously avoiding.

They met before lunch in his office, and it was the most helpful start to her return that nothing there had changed between them. Busy writing, he didn't look up as she sat down, and when he did he regarded her coolly.

"You look better. No more ideas about why you thought you knew the young man?"

"I'm afraid not."

"See if that window along the corridor has access to an accessible piece of roof. And if it's easily unlocked from the inside."

"I will."

"Someone will come for you on Friday. Take care."

"That's all, then?"

"I suppose so. You know everything."

"I wish I did."

They smiled at one another as she left the room, but she hadn't known he would be absent from the lunch table, and that she would not see him again before she went. Rupert drove her back in time for Hill House tea.

3

Matron opened the door to them, giving an immediate twist to Helen's apprehension.

"Oh, Miss Jones," said Matron impatiently. Helen was struck, as each rare time that she saw this woman, by her cold poise. Matron abstracted Miss Jones's coat, clicked her fingers and handed it to Nurse Hazel who had instantly appeared. "I'll take her through," conceded Matron briskly.

"Oh, I'll come through as well," said Rupert easily.

"If you wish." Helen was reinforced in her original feeling that this woman objected to being crossed, in however slight a way. She gave off an air of intense irritability, but also of formidable competence and, admittedly, fair dealing. "In that case, as I'm really rather busy, I'll leave her to you." Matron stretched her mouth coldly towards Rupert and went quickly away.

"Ice maiden," murmured Rupert as he took his aunt's arm. In the lounge Nurse Jackie, assisted by Miss Anthony, was wrestling to return Mrs. Charlesworth to her chair. Mrs. Charlesworth's face was distorted with malignant fury.

"Don't you look at me!" blazed Mrs. Charlesworth, at Mrs. Wellington's unblinking lizard stare. Mrs. Wellington sat a little forward, raised her clawed hand a few inches off the chair arm.

"You kicked me!" she accused. She made a token gesture of bending towards her feet.

"That was probably me, lovey." Nurse Jackie spoke as cheerily as was compatible with perching on the arm of Mrs. Charlesworth's chair and keeping a firm grip on her. On the other side Miss Anthony, still pale and expressionless, was having the same precarious success. Rupert eased Helen into Miss Jones's chair.

"You're an idiot!" announced Mrs. Charlesworth furiously. She was staring across the room now, perhaps into Miss Welch's large frightened eyes. "Don't you look at me. I'll kick you, I will. Idiot. Fool."

"We're all fools," said Mrs. Wellington loudly. In the bright room there was palpable tension. Mr. Thomas had got to his feet. Miss Protheroe was ignoring a spectacular sky to look down into her lap. Mrs. Anthony murmured softly, "Oh dear, oh dear." Miss Duncan stared at Mrs. Wellington, and there was alarm in her face. Mrs. Stoddart babbled of the soothing properties of a cup of tea.

Mrs. Wellington crouched towards her.

"Shut up! Shut up! Shut up!"

Next to Helen, the small straining movements of the nurse and Miss Anthony abruptly ceased. Turning her head she saw that Mrs. Charlesworth was once more staring fixedly ahead.

"It's all right," said Nurse Jackie gaily. She got up and Miss Anthony, shrugging, followed suit. "Thank you, Miss Anthony, you've certainly—"

"It isn't all right," cried Mrs. Wellington, trembling with feeling.

"Oh dear," said Mrs. Anthony, as her daughter took her hand.

Mrs. Wellington's face shot round.

"*You're* not the fool you look," she said to Mrs. Anthony. "And *you* Miss Jones . . ." Helen forced herself to keep her eyes on that wild unhappy gaze. "You're not either . . ."

Rupert's hand tightened on her shoulder. Miss Protheroe was looking at her, then at Rupert above her. Perhaps his knuckles were white . . . Thank heaven, Mrs. Wellington was now looking at Mr. Thomas, fixing with contempt his propitiatory smile. Between them, Mrs. Stoddart was trying to get to her feet. Nurse Jackie caught her as she began to fall.

"There we are, Mrs. Stoddart!" said Nurse Jackie. "It'll be tea-time soon."

But the fire was going out of Mrs. Wellington. She leaned back wearily and shut her eyes. Everyone except Miss Protheroe was looking at her, Miss Anthony and Miss Duncan's visitor as well. Miss Protheroe was once more looking down at her lap.

"All idiots," murmured Mrs. Wellington. "I'm not joking."

The silence made Helen think of the silence at the end of a

passage of music, when an audience wonders if it is merely a movement or the whole piece which is over. Sister Wendy broke it, by opening the door from the dining-room.

"Tea up!" called Sister Wendy. She stood in the doorway smiling round. Her smile died abruptly. "What is it?"

"Just Mrs. Charlesworth," said Nurse Jackie heartily. "And then . . ." She inclined her head towards Mrs. Wellington's chair. "Actually, it did the trick."

Mr. Weston came in, clearing his throat, followed by Mr. Corlett.

Mr. Thomas, who had been looking comparatively glum, brightened.

"Hello!" he said. "Have you come in for your teas?"

"That's right," said Mr. Weston. He cleared his throat again and Helen, watching Mrs. Wellington's rigid repose, saw the brief fury in her face.

"I must go, Mother," said Miss Anthony. "I'll come in a taxi tomorrow, and we'll go for a drive."

"That will be nice, dear."

"I apologize for the display," said Miss Duncan loudly to her visitor. But the tension had eased and Helen saw no reaction to the remark. Anyway, Mrs. Wellington was now disappearing, with assistance, into the dining-room.

"Goodbye, Auntie." Avoiding her eye, Rupert bent and kissed the corner of her mouth. For a moment she was dizzy, wondering how much she had dreamed. He patted her hand reassuringly and went out without looking back.

"Nice young man," murmured Mrs. Anthony. "Nurse, will you help me up?"

"Nice young man . . ." repeated Helen, as Nurse Jackie pushed her chair up to the table. She swung her blank gaze over the room, and it didn't appear that anyone was looking at Miss Jones with special intentness. But if anyone had, in fact, been interested in what Mrs. Wellington had said, it would scarcely show.

As for Mrs. Wellington herself, she would hardly have spoken out if she really knew anything. During tea Mrs. Wellington didn't speak, didn't raise her head from her plate,

but twice there went through her a shuddering sigh which
Helen could only believe to be involuntary, the aftermath of
the uncharacteristic leakage of her constant and constantly
suppressed rage.

Miss Duncan seemed reluctant to let the incident go and en-
deavoured to revive the tension by deprecating it. She received no support, and indeed a mild rebuke from Miss
Protheroe.

"I know, dear. But I think we should be sorry rather than
cross. It *is* difficult sometimes, but you and I are lucky ones
and perhaps we ought to remember—"

"I hardly describe myself as lucky."

Helen got up before the general exodus began, and wandered out to the kitchen. Mrs. Roberts, making pastry at the
central table, seemed pleased to see her.

"Well, now!" she said, leaning on her flour-covered hands
and smiling benevolently, "how's our little lady? Quite well
again?"

"All right . . . thank you . . ." Helen put a hand out tentatively towards Mrs. Roberts, realizing on a shaft of dismay
that Miss Jones could expect some supranormal pity from the
staff for her recent indisposition, which would mean additional
kindly scrutiny.

But Mrs. Roberts really couldn't look at her any more keenly
than she had always done. "Well, now," she said, "you don't
seem to be so bad." She glanced impatiently towards the inner
door. "Tracy O'Connor," she called out, "however long are you
going to be with that milk?"

"Milk . . . good for you . . ." murmured Miss Jones.

"Very good for you, dear. Come *on*, child!" shouted Mrs.
Roberts, and Tracy appeared with her arms full of milk bottles.

Helen drifted over to the comfortable armchair which always made her want to doze. But adrenalin flowed at the un-
precedented sight of the matron and the deputy matron entering the kitchen together.

"Mrs. Armitage and I have covered all points," said Matron

briskly to Mrs. Roberts. "I shall be back at six o'clock tomorrow evening." Matron looked at Helen merely to click her tongue.

"Enjoy yourself, Matron," said Mrs. Roberts.

"Thank you." Matron inclined her head and swiftly left the kitchen. Helen watched hopefully as Mrs. Armitage lowered herself into a chair beside the table. The scene appeared to be set for the lamentations of two fat ladies. But even as the deputy matron leaned her elbows on the table and drew breath, Mrs. Roberts gave an exaggerated start and looked at the watch nestling in the flesh of her wrist.

"Six o'clock, Mrs. Armitage! And me promising to telephone my son not a moment later! Tracy! Finish off these veggies for me, will you? And tidy up for the night when you've served the drinks, I've worked long beyond my time today as it is." She pushed Tracy away from the sink so that she could rinse her hands. "Sorry to dash off like this, Mrs. Armitage, but I'd no idea of the time."

"Of course, Mrs. Roberts, I've got to get along myself, anyway." But Helen had seen the disappointed droop to the deputy matron's mouth.

The two women left the kitchen together, and when Helen got up a few minutes later Tracy wiped her hands on her apron and took her by the arm as far as the lounge door.

Miss Jones hovered there. Everyone was present except for Messrs. Corlett and Weston, Mrs. Wayne-Jenkins and the sisters who lived upstairs. Helen went across the hall to the cloakroom, approaching her face in the mirror with the inevitable apprehension. But as always so far she was reassured. She reflected behind her impassive stare that in fact there was more reassurance in looking at Miss Jones than at Mrs. Markham. She knew how Miss Jones ought to be, while Mrs. Markham . . . She was so well disciplined, now, that although in her mind she permitted herself a smile to match her ironic thoughts, her face failed to express it, went on staring blankly back at her as if locked into its temporary identity.

Behind Miss Jones's head the door was opening and Helen very slightly altered the direction of her stare. It was Mr.

Thomas, his hands already at his trousers, but jerking away with the residual reflex of the gentleman. Or the calculation of another actor?

She half-turned and murmured, staring past him, "I was just thinking . . ."

"Good evening, Miss Jones."

Mr. Thomas was smiling his usual leisurely smile, but perhaps he was really in a hurry. Miss Jones was scarcely up to making a gesture towards the inner doors, or going to the exit while Mr. Thomas was barring it. But she could sit down on the cork chair. Murmuring now unintelligibly, Helen did so, and Mr. Thomas continued to stand just inside the cloakroom door, smiling at her.

"I think it's really been a very nice day."

He made the remark, in the same friendly and conversational tone, three times, shuffling very slightly forward as he spoke. His eye was hypnotic, but Miss Jones didn't catch people's eyes.

"Nice day . . ." she repeated twice, and the third time she said "Julian . . ." and he said "I went out to tea with my daughter," and they lapsed into silence, respectively smiling and staring, and she heard the water moving in the pipes, saw and heard a bee struggling angrily against the imprisoning frosted window, was stiff and scared. Such dogged patience could of course be in the nature of Mr. Thomas's breakdown, but it could also be an attempt at the breakdown of Mr. Jones's agent, this friendly, radiant smile which seemed to illumine and reveal her in an unnaturally bright light. But she couldn't get out of it and she couldn't turn it off . . .

"I wonder if it'll be sunny tomorrow?"

Mr. Thomas shuffled a little bit nearer and she faltered that she didn't know, clutching her bag with one hand and covering her clenched knuckles with the other. The end came because the door opened from outside, hitting Mr. Thomas in the back and in a second precipitating him further forward than he had moved in all the time he and Helen had been regarding one another.

"Well, now," said Sister Wendy, "what, may I ask, is this?"

"I was telling Miss Jones," said Mr. Thomas, "that it's really been a very nice day."

"You tell her in the lounge," said Sister Wendy, "and give Mrs. Stoddart a chance."

"I'm just going in here." Mr. Thomas lurched into a cubicle. Sister Wendy manœuvred Mrs. Stoddart into another. Her large-faced wristwatch showed that the ordeal had lasted almost half an hour.

CHAPTER 11

1

Back in the lounge the company sat motionless and unresponding as bullets whined across the television screen, through the length of an ancient Western, in an absurd parody of Helen's grimmest expectations. As the evening ground slowly on her unease and frustration concentrated in a furious urge to perform the simplest of operations—to take the few steps necessary to turn the set off. The film was almost over by the time Sister Wendy came in and decided nobody was watching. Helen put out a hand to the crisp apron as it bustled by, crackling in the restored silence.

"You ready for bed, then, Miss Jones?"

"Yes. Want to go to bed."

Oh, Julian. He had taught her so well there were stretches of time, at Hill House, when she wasn't consciously aware of him, and then when she was she must refuse to drown in the wave of incredulous joy which overwhelmed her.

"Julian takes me upstairs. Julian . . ."

It was the only safe way to express her inward smile.

"You've a good brother," said Sister Wendy. Sufficiently articulate for the moment, Helen mumbled a response. Upstairs, left to herself in what was still her own room, she took her dress off and walked about. When she had reluctantly put on Miss Jones's nightgown she stood at the window and watched the last of the pink light fade from sky and sea, straining her eyes to the horizon.

There were so many ordinary things as yet unsavoured—like walking with Julian on the shore—that the temptation to day-dream was as dangerous as the temptation to reminisce. The only thing was to keep reminding herself of the unpleasant fact that if she wasn't vigilant these things would never hap-pen. Particularly if the young man came back and she wasn't ready . . . Anyway, she wanted to complete the task Julian had set her, that desire was as strong as any other . . .

It was almost dark when she got into bed. She lay down to rest, too alert in her happiness and apprehension to be afraid that sleep would overtake her. The texture of the night was thin and when she got up again she could read the clock by the grey oblong of the window. It was almost midnight, and she drifted out of the room.

She could see faces where they lay close to other thinly cur-tained windows. Miss Protheroe was curled up small on her side. Her breathing was so faint Helen must lean almost cheek to cheek to catch the infinitesimal rhythm. Beyond her, less detailed in the shadow, Mrs. Charlesworth lay rigid on her back, her sharp features pointed at the ceiling. Helen picked up a glass from the locker beside Mrs. Anthony's bed, looking out under her lids as she bent her head to examine it. Mrs. An-thony was lying on her side, her back to the wall, her face but for its closed eyes exactly its amiable daytime self, her breath-ing quiet but noticeable. There was nothing on the locker ex-cept the glass, nothing at all on Mrs. Charlesworth's. It was perhaps the saddest thing of all that these people had so little left of their own. Nothing, really.

She stood in the doorway of the peaceful room, fighting what could turn out to be her worst enemy—an expectancy of failure. And with it self-distrust, against which the only weapon was to think of the skill with which she knew she was playing her part. A skill which she must concede to her no doubt professional opponent . . .

The door of the men's room was ajar. She could make out the flat oblong of the empty bed, the dromedary hump of Mr. Corlett's small plump body, the bactrian peaks of Mr. Thomas. Mr. Weston's bed in the darkest corner seemed to be empty too . . .

It would have been worse if there had been any warning, if she had heard footsteps behind her. As it was, one second she was peering towards Mr. Weston's bed, and the next the assault was taking place behind her, pushing her hard against the door so that it swung back to its fullest extent, protesting. Unhurt but waiting for pain or oblivion, Helen heard the muttered curse, felt the hands at her elbows, made herself look up.

Mr. Weston's face was on a level with hers, very close and looking at her with a sort of rueful curiosity.

"Sorry, old girl." Mr. Weston dropped his hands and retied the knot of his pyjama cord. He cleared his throat, smiled nervously, cleared his throat. "The old waterworks not what they were. Didn't hurt you, did I? Rather think you scared me more than I scared you."

Helen could hardly agree with him. Beyond them Mr. Thomas muttered and stirred. Mr. Weston once more took her by the elbows and walked her a few steps until they stood clear of the bedroom door. There he hesitated and Miss Jones began to turn away.

"All right, then," said Mr. Weston. She thought his face brightened in relief as he shuffled back into the bedroom. The door creaked as he pushed it to, she heard him clear his throat again, and then there was silence except for the noisy pounding of her heart . . .

Miss Jones teetered along the landing, and beyond the next door there was a voice. Helen entered the room and stood listening as her eyes adjusted to another pattern of gloom. The voice was unfamiliar, an attractive low female voice murmuring recognizable phrases.

"You know I don't want you to go . . . Don't make me stay behind, let me come with you . . . I may never see you again . . . I can't bear it . . . Can't bear . . . Can't . . ."

Miss Welch's bed was beside the window, and it was Miss Welch speaking these sane if agitated words. The voice was unfamiliar because in the daytime the two or three words which under persuasion Miss Welch put together came out as a barely comprehensible singsong.

It was a moment which had to be exploited. Evoking the protection of her role, Helen put out a fluttery hand and let it fall on Miss Welch's forehead.

The skin under her trembling fingers was hot and dry. As Helen moved her hand Miss Welch started and opened her eyes—and saw the person she was talking to.

It was as if she was in normal contact with someone standing where I was standing. But as I stroked her forehead her eyes went blank, and her face, and there was no one else there. She stared through me in her usual terrified way, and then her eyes closed. Either I had witnessed a phenomenal reversion to normality induced by a dream, or Miss Welch is a consummate operator. I incline to the former theory . . .

Nevertheless Helen sank into a chair while her own agitation subsided. The second bed in the room was empty, and she sat in a silence for perhaps ten minutes, and Miss Welch neither moved nor spoke. Looking down on her before drifting out of the room, Helen saw that every muscle in her face seemed to be locked back into terror, even as she slept and breathed with the gentle rhythm of the dreamless sleeper. Helen found herself with the same almost indignant conviction of innocence she had felt for the legless Mrs. Harvey. But *nothing is obvious, Mrs. Markham . . .*

Sounds came from the small room where Mrs. Wellington slept alone, unidentifiable until Helen was standing by the bed. Then she found that Mrs. Wellington appeared to be very softly and steadily weeping. Her head was turned away from the door, her face was buried in the sheet, and the small dismal sound went on and on. Remembering the acuteness of Mrs. Wellington's ears, Helen picked up the glass half full of water on the bedside locker and set it sharply down, and Mrs. Wellington was sitting up, stabbing forward with her clawlike hand.

The fingernails grated down the brushed nylon of Helen's nightdress. The curtains were back and Mrs. Wellington stared at her, hostile and defiant, in the grey light of the window. The side of her face where the light fell glinted wet beneath the eye. She looked even more ill than by day.

"You're useless," said Mrs. Wellington sullenly. "Useless. Go away." However, she went on looking hungrily at Helen, and Helen felt sorry rather than afraid. She moved only as far as Mrs. Wellington's armchair, which faced the bed. Mrs. Wellington stared at her for a further moment of mingled anger and entreaty, then plunged down into the bed again. It seemed that she had rendered herself defenceless. There was no further sound from her, beyond an occasional shuddery sob, and no reaction when Helen got to her feet, deliberately stumbling, and left the room.

Unless Mrs. Wellington had been out of bed, following my progress, she could hardly have staged her tears . . .

Mrs. Stoddart's sleep was punctuated by tiny regular snores. She lay on her back with her head off the pillow. Miss Duncan was on her stomach with her arms raised each side of her head. On her locker the complete works of Tennyson lay beneath a paperback detective story.

She had wakened both ladies before, without advantage, she had seen almost everything she had seen tonight on other nights, and she went out on to the landing imagining the relief of putting back her head and howling, as much from the depression of her tour in its insistent illustration of life's dying fall as from the frustration of her job. Of all her regular activities, the one she had most to steel herself to was her nocturnal round of her fellow patients . . .

In the dim glow of the landing light she saw the yellow line round Mrs. Wayne-Jenkins's door. Helen tried the door and it opened silently and she crept across the carpet to the desk and the pool of lamplight which illumined it. Mrs. Wayne-Jenkins was sitting at the desk, writing with apparent absorp-

tion. Two large sheets of typing paper had been covered with
bold black writing and pushed aside. At the top of one of them,
in capital letters, were the words *My Life and Times* by Sarah
Wayne-Jenkins.

Helen leaned from behind the authoress and took hold of
the corner of the sheet on which she was engaged. Mrs.
Wayne-Jenkins uttered a quavering moan and slumped back
in her chair. She had removed the look of health which she
wore during the day (peach-coloured cotton-wool was always
to be found in her wastepaper basket) and her yellow skin
was mottled beige. Helen moved forward in an alarm which
she had to struggle to keep out of her face, into Mrs. Wayne-
Jenkins's direct view, and was weak with the relief of seeing
robust fury in the suddenly crimson features.

Mrs. Wayne-Jenkins was on her feet.

"You silly bitch!"

She had Helen by the wrist and it hurt. Miss Jones whimpered. Mrs. Wayne-Jenkins let go with a push which sent Helen
stumbling across the room, and marched over to the bell.

*Yet another incident to reinforce my impression that with
Mrs. Wayne-Jenkins things are what they seem.*

Nurse Sandra was there almost at once.

"Oh dear me, Miss Jones, we do seem to upset the applecart,
don't we?"

"It really is too bad, Nurse!"

"I know, Mrs. Wayne-Jenkins, I'm sorry. Has she done this
before?"

The crimson flowed briefly back.

"I am generally asleep at this time. She hasn't wakened me,
no. But that is hardly the point."

"Of course not. I'll have a word with Matron. I'm so sorry,
Mrs. Wayne-Jenkins. Come along now, Miss Jones. Dear me, I
was just on my way to see Mrs. Lambert."

"Come with you," said Miss Jones, while Helen tried to accommodate the uncomfortable implication of Nurse Sandra's
words.

"All right, you come with me."

Mrs. Harvey appeared to be asleep. Mrs. Lambert as always

held out her arms to Miss Jones, who sat down on the chair farthest from the bed, coughing into her hand. When the nurse had finished she escorted Miss Jones back to her room, and inside. Helen sat down on the edge of her bed and after hovering in a moment's indecision Nurse Sandra said "Good night, Miss Jones" with unaccustomed severity and left.

Helen went on sitting on the edge of the bed, trembling from head to foot, fighting an attack of fear. Fear that her judgement had failed her, that she had destroyed her scope— Nurse Sandra had been in two minds whether to wait until her awkward charge was actually in bed, until she appeared to be asleep perhaps, she could have taken it on herself to lock the bedroom door. *I'll have a word with Matron.*

Fear that the young man would come while she was sitting there afraid.

Fear that her fear could turn into a loss of nerve.

2

It was three o'clock before she was fit to leave the room again, and that was to carry out the most simple of Mr. Jones's injunctions: to see if the window along the corridor gave on to a stretch of roof.

She opened the door and listened before coming out on to the landing. It was an added hazard to be afraid, now, of meeting Nurse Sandra. But the oblique view of the night nurses' little room, glowing gold in the gloom, showed her drooping beside the desk in an attitude of sleep.

Helen flitted across the landing and drifted the length of the corridor beyond it. The kitchen door was ajar and so was the window, the bottom sash raised just enough for her to see the sloping glisten of the roof outside. If only there was something for her to pick up and examine while she was examining what she could see through the window. *In character at all times, Mrs. Markham, when there is the possibility of observation—*

One hand fell on her shoulder, the other on her arm. She and the person behind her stood very still and then Miss Jones began feebly to struggle and to mutter her rhymes.

"You again, I see. You've saved me the trouble, my dear. I was just on my way to your room."

The voice was unusual, at the same time gruff and squeaky. How could such a voice sound familiar?

She was being spun round, was facing her assailant, was in a more painful dual grip. The moustache masked the expression of the young man's mouth, but the eyes were pale and cold as they searched her face.

"Mary had a little lamb. Mary had. *Had!*"

"Am I hurting you, my dear? Do tell me if I'm hurting you. If you can tell me. Can you?"

There was after all an expression in the eyes, a mingling of curiosity and enjoyment. Her arm was up her back, stinging and burning against her body.

"Hickory dickory dock. Hickorydickorydock!"

Miss Jones panted and moaned, Helen knew what she looked like, head threshing from side to side like the head of a trapped animal, then suddenly jerking up and the eyes staring without understanding into those opaque pebbles . . .

"Mary had a little lamb. *L-a-amb!*"

She couldn't take any more pain without fighting, without looking and hating, she couldn't. But she was doing. "Mary had, Mary had, Mary had . . ." Perhaps the repetition was helping Helen Markham as well, go on using it, use it like a totem. "Little lamb, little lamb . . ." Lamb of God. Dear God.

The grip was still strong but the eyes were no longer curious and the pain was very slightly less. She had managed it, she knew she had managed it. Confidence flowed back with the realization, overcoming her fear. And gratitude, that the encounter had not been in the irremediable intimacy of her bedroom . . .

As if in recognition of her gratitude, over her assailant's shoulder she saw a female figure in a dressing-gown slouch out of the staff bathroom, yawning hugely. One moment Tracy was standing there, rubbing her eyes, the next she was behind the young man, was kneeing him viciously in the lower back so that he flew past Miss Jones and through the open door of the kitchen, his face violently against the table, his feet as he

staggered to his knees scrunching in the glass of the milk bottle which had been shaken to the floor.

"That was your bad luck," said Tracy. "I took evening
classes in female self-defence. I'm going to ring the police."
Miss Jones stood whimpering in the circle of Tracy's arm,
and Helen saw the sudden wavery red line on the young man's
left hand as he raised it to his cheek, saw the line thicken from
the base of the centre nail, along the finger, across the back of
the hand to the wrist. Saw the spilled milk streaked pink at his
feet, that he seemed unable to get up . . .

There was a whirlwind, a blow, an agonizing thud. Helen as
well as Miss Jones was uncomprehending. As she crawled to
her knees half way up the corridor the second denim leg was
disappearing through the wide window and Tracy was picking
herself up off the floor, was standing undecided, shrugging,
shutting and locking the window.

"You all right, Miss Jones? Let me look." Tracy had lifted
her up and was examining her arm, already swollen and
discoloured. "Nothing broken," said Tracy matter-of-factly.
"Now I'm going to make us both a nice cup of sweet tea, and
then take you back to bed."

Tracy didn't seem to be frightened, or even upset. Or showing any signs of raising the alarm or going to the telephone.
Miss Jones sat at the kitchen table, holding her arm and whimpering—two Miss Jones gestures which were as near as any
had been to the inclinations of Helen Markham—while Tracy
cleared all traces of glass, milk and blood from the floor, made
tea, and sat down on the other side of the table while they
both drank it.

"Least said soonest mended," said Tracy, looking keenly
round the little room before taking Miss Jones by her good
arm back to her bedroom. She stayed in the doorway until
Helen was lying down in bed.

The throbbing of her arm, then, made it seem like the major
part of her body, and she couldn't know whether it was willpower or weariness which sank her to sleep.

She woke because of the pain, which she thought was getting worse because she was dreaming the young man was still

twisting her arm. But how could he be twisting her arm if he was over by her dressing-table, opening a drawer, rummaging, taking something out, looking towards her, very softly shutting the drawer, opening another, glancing over his shoulder . . .

"*Hickorydickorydock!*"

Something fell to the ground from the man's hand as he swung round, clearing his throat.

"I say, old girl, I'm sorry . . . didn't mean . . ."

Mr. Weston was ambling towards her bed, tightening the cord of his dressing-gown, in the grey light she could see the shine of his anxious, puzzled eyes.

"Julian . . . I don't . . . See-saw, Margery Daw!"

"Look here, old girl, I didn't mean any harm. Just going to put it back. See!" Mr. Weston plunged his hand into the deep pocket of his dressing-gown and brought out Miss Jones's powder compact. The next moment, from his other capacious pocket, Mr. Weston was extracting Miss Duncan's latest detective paperback.

Mr. Weston put the powder compact and the book down on Miss Jones's bed.

"There you are, old girl. See. Not stealing, just having a look. Very sorry. But you'll understand, won't you? Oh, but of course—" Mr. Weston paused to clear his throat—"you won't understand . . . You can't . . . I say, I really am sorry . . ."

Mr. Weston appeared to be more sorry about overestimating Miss Jones's intelligence than about purloining her belongings. Still murmuring, he turned away and Miss Jones said, pettishly emphatic, "Put back! Want . . . put back . . ."

Her own powder compact and Miss Duncan's book on her coverlet were in total violation of the predictable habits of Miss Jones. And for Miss Jones to put them back could be, despite Helen Markham's instincts, to give herself up into the hands of a man who was anything but a petty thief.

To her infinite relief Mr. Weston had turned back to the bed.

"What's that?"

"Put back!"

"Of course, old girl, of course. See . . ." Mr. Weston picked up the powder compact and went over to the dressing-table. He put it slowly down, then bent and retrieved from the floor what looked like Miss Jones's hairbrush, setting it beside the compact. While Helen held her breath he came back to the bed again and picked up Miss Duncan's book.

"Good night, old girl, just going to give this back to Miss Duncan. Said she'd lend it to me, y'know. Can't always sleep. But put it back now and take it again in the morning. Better. But you'll understand . . . Sorry, old girl, of course you won't . . . can't . . . Good night. . ."

Mr. Weston had reached the door, and shuffled out.

The man with a sense of purpose. The bed shook, as Helen subdued her hysterical laughter, and then she wanted to cry. She lay for a time, forcing herself to write a mental page for Mr. Jones.

I must accept that having failed with the physical approach —I know it failed—"they" may now have tried the psychological, but all my instincts tell me that Mr. Weston is what he seems, a petty pilferer. Or perhaps a species of kleptomaniac whose compulsion is intermittent, as I do not think he had been in my room before . . .

But her attention was wandering. Why had Tracy encountered the young man as an enemy? If he wasn't a part of the establishment, who else was interested in Hill House? Unless Julian . . .

The pain in her arm would perhaps be more bearable with some outside distraction. And Miss Jones's nightgown had long sleeves.

Nurse Sandra was still dozing, and jerked awake. Her immediate reaction was annoyance, resumed from the early part of the night. It seemed extraordinary to Helen that this was the same night in which she had disturbed Mrs. Wayne-Jenkins. She sat down in the little arm chair.

"Nice girl . . ."

"I know you can't help it, but you really are an awful bloodly nuisance." Helen felt Nurse Sandra's exasperation shredding away. "If only I could get through to you—"

"How are you, I hope . . ."

"Oh, I don't know!" Nurse Sandra yawned vigorously. "Anyway, I expect Wayne-J will have a word with Matron herself."

Pain and weariness took the menace out of the remark. Miss Jones took a shuddering breath.

"Has she caught a cold, then?" Nurse Sandra by now was almost affectionate. She put out a hand and touched Helen's cheek. She yawned again, peering bleary-eyed towards the landing.

"What's the time?"

"Bedtime for you. Lucky sod." Nurse Jackie, slouching through the doorway, was even more obviously sleepy. "Hello, pet." Her face twitched in the direction of Miss Jones, not under sufficient waking control to marshal a full expression. Helen waited for what Nurse Sandra retained of the early part of the night.

"She disturbed old Wayne-J," said Nurse Sandra conversationally, getting slowly to her feet and stretching tall. "I wish she wouldn't for her own sake. It would be awful to lock her in."

"Gosh, awful!" Nurse Jackie's rubber features just registered dismay. "I mean, she's *got* to wander about. Let's not say anything. This time."

"Let's not," agreed Nurse Sandra. "Only old Wayne-J's bound to . . ."

Her voice trailed behind her from the landing. Helen heard her dragging feet quicken towards the corridor. Nurse Jackie was pressing a spot out at the side of her nose, leaning in to the ill-lit mirror over the desk.

Helen wavered to her feet.

"That's right," said Nurse Jackie nasally, not pausing in her task. "You go and get all nice and comfy in the lounge. Hell, no, I mean go back to bed for goodness' sake and wait for your breakfast!"

Another short sleep produced no dreams, and a blessed diminution of the pain. An examination of her arm suggested it had now reached its peak of size and coloration, and she was able to swathe it in Miss Jones's sleeve without too much discomfort. But she was still tired and after breakfast she made straight for the kitchen and Mrs. Roberts's armchair. There was absolutely no reason why she should feel safest, most sparing of nervous energy, in the kitchen. But she did.

3

Mrs. Roberts and Tracy were both there to greet her, Tracy her usual untidy daytime self, hair straggling out from under her cap, her face pink and shiny.

"You all right, pet?"

Mrs. Roberts could have been looking at Miss Jones even more carefully than usual. Helen saw Tracy's swift glance towards her employer. Then Tracy had turned back to the sink and Mrs. Roberts was taking off her overall, hanging it in its usual place.

"I'm going up to see Mrs. Armitage. You get on with that still-room, Tracy O'Connor!"

"Just on my way, Mrs. Roberts."

Tracy slopped through the inner doorway. Mrs. Roberts patted her hair in the mirror, turned round, took a couple of steps forward, then turned slowly back. She touched the overall, looked towards the still-room door, towards Miss Jones, put her hand back on the overall, specifically this time on the overall pocket, looked again towards Miss Jones, this time with a cheerful smile, shrugged, and went quickly out of the room. She had no sooner gone than the gestures Helen had just witnessed seemed infinitesimal, imagined almost, it seemed absurd to have so much as been aware of them.

But the white overall behind the inner door seemed to dominate the whole large room.

Beyond the door Tracy could be heard and intermittently seen, slowly wet-mopping the tiles. Miss Jones got up from the armchair, advanced to the kitchen table, picked a biscuit from a plate, wavered across to the door . . . Well behind it, out of sight of Tracy. The smallest gesture necessary, to touch the top of the pocket, feel the stiffness of the paper inside it, draw the paper up. And even if Tracy came back into the kitchen, Miss Jones opened drawers, examined things . . .

Tracy, or her mop, had knocked the metal bucket, making it dismally clang. The paper seemed to be a dozen or so sheets of letterhead. Hill House, and the address. Nothing else in the pocket. A choking mouthful of biscuit. All the sheets the same. Some words, very small, at the bottom.

Printed by Her Majesty's Stationery Office.

Tucking the paper back inside the overall pocket was a lifetime of frenzied thinking, crazily shifting horizons. Hill House on one side, Julian on the other. One the enemy, one the ally. Anyone whose letterhead was printed by Her Majesty's Stationery Office must be the ally, and so Julian . . . It was all, of course, as Julian had said it was, except that The Laurels and Hill House were the other way round. And one person was carrying loyalty as far as it would go, as she had been tricked into carrying treason . . .

Hardly knowing what she did, she wandered through the inner door.

"You going to walk on my nice clean floor, then?" Tracy greeted her good-humouredly. Helen crossed the floor and held out an aimless hand to this handle, to that. The larder door was open, she recognized the chop which Mrs. Stoddart had left on her plate the day before, and was shocked by another onslaught of hysterical laughter.

"I hope you haven't caught a cold, Miss Jones." Tracy thumped her affectionately on the back.

"Nice girl . . ."

Helen drifted out of the still-room, went out of the kitchen. She paused in the lounge doorway and looked dazedly round. Miss Protheroe in her seat by the window, Miss Welch staring agonized across the room. Mrs. Charlesworth and Mrs. Anthony respectively blank and amiable of expression. Mr. Thomas standing in front of Mrs. Anthony, in sluggishly flowing monologue. Mrs. Wellington with closed eyes, Miss Duncan apparently absorbed in a book. Mrs. Stoddart, with equal concentration, picking at a frayed edge of fabric on the arm of her chair.

The same and yet, like everything else in the world, no longer in any way the same.

The agent of a foreign power. I, Helen Markham. Each part of the picture had to change, including her own portrait. Portrait of a lady. Portrait of a fool. Portrait of a spy. Well, she had been that all along.

She could be the agent of a foreign power, and Julian would have made her so. She had asked so little of Julian, and he had perhaps taken from her the most that could be taken from anyone.

Yet whatever side he was on, he had had no need to make her more than his agent. What she had learned in the last few hours had no bearing on him and her.

But it did. It was as terrible to betray loyalty as to betray love. To make people do things for which they would never be able to forgive themselves.

"Don't you want any lunch today, Miss Jones, love?"

Nurse Hazel had her on her feet with a cool firm arm. Mrs. Stoddart was disappearing through the dining-room doorway and the lounge was empty. While she had been wrestling with herself she had perhaps missed something . . .

What could she have missed? Her reflexes were working . . . Julian had sent in his young man again, the young man he had pretended to be perturbed about, the young man who had enjoyed hurting her. And the only living-in spy was herself, searching for something which would enable her to betray her country. And now—the latest revelation locked her rigid in her seat—having to decide whether to report to her employer or to his enemy . . .

"Come on, then, Miss Jones, lovey, aren't we hungry today? Look at Mrs. Anthony, she's finished!"

"Nice girl . . ."

And definitely less frightening now. But that was ridiculous. They were on opposing sides. And Julian had shown her . . .

No, no, no. It was no good thinking of Julian in a panelled office with people round him speaking in public school voices. Kim Philby had had those. And anyway she had only to set the picture beside the memory of a sheet of paper with a line of print it had not been known she would see.

And beside Tracy fighting the young man who had hurt her. The young man was Tracy's enemy. And so . . .

All sense of urgency seemed to have gone. Together with the surge of her happiness, which in the perspective of merely a few hours seemed to shine with an innocent brilliance. Only her training now, and habit, were carrying her along. And would do so more safely, perhaps, without the tension, the anxiety to get it right. She wanted to laugh again, at herself this time, and coughed into her bib.

"You all right, Miss Jones?"

She might feel safer, but there was still an enemy, even if it was only herself. Helen picked up Miss Duncan's napkin ring and examined it before getting up and drifting out to the kitchen. She was sitting there when Sister Wendy came to tell her that her brother had arrived.

CHAPTER 12

1

She couldn't look for him. She wasn't sure where he would be waiting, and, leaning on Sister Wendy's arm, she kept her eyes on the carpet from the moment they left the kitchen.

It was only the discipline of her role which made her raise her eyes from the familiar feet, standing outside the lounge door, and stare him in the face.

He looked back with his usual lightly concerned affection.

"Hello, sweetheart." And to Sister Wendy, "How is she?"

"I think she's just fine, Mr. Jones. A wee bit reluctant with her lunch today, perhaps, but it may be the spring. She ate it all up in the end."

"That's the ticket."

It was all so reflex, it must come off the very top of his head. He went the other side of her, took her other arm, and it glowed defiant of her and of her injury, under his touch. She could still see him in her mind's eye, as he had just that moment looked, the only face there was, blotting out her view of the room, her view of how she ought to behave, everything except himself.

The extra chair was brought up and he held her hand in his lap, caressing it. She didn't bother any more to block off her awareness of the contact, concentrate instead on what other people in the room were doing. All she noticed was that the tall handsome Mrs. Winters, Mrs. Wellington's daughter, was going through her usual ritual of apparently having to persuade her mother to undertake a run in the car, and that Miss Anthony hadn't come. Mrs. Anthony complained gently to Sister Wendy, who perched on the arm of her chair.

"I'm sorry, lovey. She *was* coming, you're quite right, but she doesn't feel so well today, and she's leaving it till tomorrow. She'll be here without fail tomorrow. A promise."

"Yes. I know she will." There was the suspicion of a tremor in Mrs. Anthony's voice. "She's a very good daughter."

Yesterday Miss Jones would probably have murmured an agreement. Today Helen pressed Julian's fingers in her palm and he said, easily but instantly, "Well, dear, it's not a bad sort of a day. We'll go down to the pier at Boscombe, eh, and look for ice-cream?"

"Julian, I don't know . . ."

He was helping her to her feet. Mrs. Anthony's mouth went into a pout.

"You're lucky," she said.

"Some people have all the luck." Mrs. Wellington, her arguments overborne, was just leaving the room with her daughter, but she turned back to make the statutory comment. Helen wondered how many times she had heard Mrs. Wellington make it. She was wondering about everything except what she must say to Julian. She shouldn't have pressed his hand, she had nothing worked out, she should have let his unexpected visit come and go in the lounge. But she couldn't wait, she couldn't go on feeling what he had done to her and not face him with it, she couldn't help looking in the only possible place where there might be a crumb of comfort. And if there wasn't, to let him see she was no longer an ignorant fool . . .

Mrs. Stoddart leaned perilously forward in her chair. "You'll be having tea out, Miss Jones?"

"No, she'll be back for tea," reported Mr. Jones cheerily. "Come along, sweetheart."

When they reached the door Miss Protheroe waved a hand round in the air without taking her eyes off the window. On the threshold Mr. Corlett apologized profusely for occupying the narrow space at the same time. Behind him Mr. Weston cleared his throat, then cleared it again. Everything the same, and yet not at all the same.

In the hall the deputy matron was talking to Mrs. Wellington's daughter. She responded noticeably to the sight of Mr. Jones. Helen's response to the sight of the deputy matron bridling self-consciously was to realize that she could be jealous. The reaction was so inappropriate she had to turn yet another laugh into a cough.

"Not getting a cold, are we?" asked the deputy matron automatically. "Whether or not," she said to Mr. Jones, "I think we should have our coat."

"Undoubtedly." His voice was courteously grave.

Nurse Jackie was reaching the foot of the stairs.

"Oh, Nurse," said Mrs. Armitage. "I'm sorry, but can you just run upstairs again and fetch Miss Jones's coat?"

Unsmilingly Nurse Jackie turned and began a plodding ascent. For the lengthy few moments before the coat was delivered, Mrs. Armitage looked at Mr. Jones and talked to him. After her first stare, Helen hadn't looked at him again. The deputy matron insisted on their waiting yet another few moments while she sent Nurse Jackie for a handful of tissues against the ice-cream. Helen wondered, as Mrs. Armitage saw them personally into the car, how many times in her own life she had unknowingly been an irrelevance on the surface of other people's dramas.

Mrs. Wayne-Jenkins was on the lawn, nodding impatiently. Helen's mental picture of her in a flowered dressing-gown, writing, seemed to come from far away in the past. It wasn't that she wouldn't speak, on the way down to the pier, it was that she couldn't, she could only wait for Julian to say something, and then find out how she was going to respond. But he said nothing either, and when he stopped outside the ice-cream shop the silence between them was still unbroken.

They sat motionless, staring ahead. He said at last, softly, "What's the matter?"

Her heart leapt, but she ignored it. She said, as quietly, "I haven't put on my usual performance today, then?"

He made an uncharacteristic sharp movement. "Of course you have. I just feel—"

"You're so aware of me? I'll have strawberry today."

He jerked again. "Yes. In a moment. There was no need for me to come today."

"No?"

"No. Therefore, as there was no need to come, I should not have come."

She recognized one of the unwritten rules.

"So?"

He said even more softly, "I wanted to see you."

"There was hardly a risk."

She felt, rather than heard, his sigh.

"No. But there is always a slight lip to a slippery slope, and one is already on dangerous ground if one decides to venture—"

"Yes. Thank you." If she hadn't read those words, how happy she would be! "I appreciate that you wanted to see me, and so you came."

Appreciate it! The knowledge of it was flooding through her, warming her, filling her with uncomfortable delight . . .

But she couldn't trust him. She knew, now, with what pains and brilliance he could lie.

He said drily, "I'm glad you appreciate it."

She said, without deciding to say it, "It's as well you came, for whatever reason. I have some important things to say to you. Better get the ice-creams."

She couldn't keep the cold out of her voice and she could feel the probe of his gaze, but she had to go on staring straight ahead. It seemed a long time before he gave up trying to will her face round towards him, and got out of the car. He had forgotten to open the window, which gave her a stab of pleasure, and surreptitiously she wound it down. She turned to look at him as he came out of the shop, and saw, first in his movement with the ice-cream cornets, then in his eyes, his reaction to his oversight and her correction of it.

"Here you are, Helen."

He handed a cornet in. He had also forgotten to arrange any tissues round her neck or in her lap. She held the cornet unlicked until he had got into the car and made good his second lapse.

"Well?" he said, as coldly as she, leaning back in his seat. They were both looking straight ahead.

"I found some sheets of paper."

"I beg your pardon?"

"In an overall pocket. Some sheets of writing paper. Headed Hill House. Published by Her Majesty's Stationery Office."

She turned to him at last, to study his face. Even from Julian, now, she expected some evidence of anger or alarm, but he appeared to be merely surprised. She almost thought that a smile lurked. Well, it could be a sporting smile, at the fate which had betrayed him in so subtle yet so sure a way.

Rather an old-fashioned attitude. Which Julian was, of course. Which the whole world was in which he moved and had his being, since its needs and urgencies couldn't alter from week to week.

"Well, now," he said.

"Published by Her Majesty's Stationery Office," repeated Helen. "I don't have to explain to you how I feel."

"You don't, of course not. And I think, now, you should stop looking at me so super intelligently and resume the trappings of your role."

"It doesn't come quite so obediently any more." If Julian

wasn't angry, she was, that he hardly seemed to find it important for her to have discovered what he had done to her. Nevertheless she turned away from him and stared vacantly
through the windscreen. Without moving her head Helen
wound up the window. "That isn't the only thing."

"Good heavens!"

She ignored his tone. "The young man did come back.
Thank God I met him in the corridor and not in the bedroom.
Tracy appeared and knocked him for six. Then he knocked
Tracy down and went through the corridor window. But you
know."

"And how do I know?"

Still the same controlled yet intense curiosity, she was sure
of it, instantly there was a mention of the young man.

"Because you sent him in."

"Oh, Helen." She had a sudden leaping hope that his
lightness of manner was a shield for hurt. "If I sent him in,
why haven't I put him to work with you?"

She felt a shrug, but her training held her back from expressing it in her shoulders.

"Perhaps your left hand and your right hand are playing
different games. How should I know? I only know that he's
Tracy's enemy. And so . . ."

She waited in longing for an explanation, but he only said,
after a pause, "Tracy knocked him down?"

She said wearily, "Sent him flying from behind. He was
hurting my arm."

"Let me see!" At last there was the possibility of concern.
She held out her arm, and he pulled up coat and dress sleeves
to reveal the rich distortion. As he saw it an indefinable expression crossed his face.

"He enjoyed himself," said Helen, "but it's all right, it hardly
hurts me now. And I know for sure that he still thinks I'm
Miss Jones. And he didn't get off scot free, he fell against the
table in the little kitchen and knocked a milk bottle off, then
fell on to the broken glass." If only there would be some kind
of readable expression in his face. "Julian, I can't think or feel
as I did. You must realize that."

"I realize—of course I do. And I realize I have to ask you to trust me."

"I did trust you." To her fury she heard a tremor in her voice.

"I know." His hands came over to her, and she found she had finished her ice-cream. He talked as he tidied her up. "And now you feel . . . I'm not happy about how you feel."

"You could have fooled me." She hated to hear herself flip, but that was how anger tended to make her. "If I say that I won't go back, now?"

She was afraid of him, and had to test her fear. Afraid of Julian. But there had never been a time, really, when she hadn't in a way been afraid of him, of the extent of his power.

"I would try to reason with you and then, if you still said you would betray me, or not work for me any more, I should have to take you back to The Laurels."

"I don't think you're the one to talk about betrayal." The menace of his quiet words had touched her with physical fear. And already he was a stranger. Even before he took his hands away, he and she were far apart.

"So you think I've outdone the phoney agent in your film?"

"What else can I think?"

"And now your faith is in Hill House."

"I don't know where my faith is. But I know Hill House's writing paper is printed by Her Majesty's Stationery Office. No chance that could have been laid on for me. Nobody would know that I'd looked in an overall pocket."

"I accept that. Whose pocket?"

"Oh no, Julian, I'm not going to tell you that."

"Helen—this is absurd."

"I agree. You should be at least as angry as I am."

"I'm not angry, for God's sake, I'm anxious. For you not to—hurt yourself. To go on trusting me. I give you my solemn word that I haven't betrayed your trust, however it may look. And that I never will."

"That's all you're prepared to give? Forgive me if it doesn't seem like very much."

She hoped his sudden movement meant he was wincing.

"It's all I can give you at the moment."

His voice now was serious, yet she still felt his anxiety was short of total. If he was deceiving her, and wanted to go on deceiving her, wouldn't he be trying harder, turning in a more convincing performance?

"I can't," she said slowly, "feel you're as worried as I'd expect you to be by what I've found out."

He laughed, abruptly cut it off.

"You think I'm being complacent in believing you wouldn't reveal yourself to the clients of Her Majesty's Stationery Office without first warning me?"

"I haven't gone to them, no. But I feel safer at Hill House than I did."

"Helen, for God's sake!"

For the first time there was full concern. She turned to him at the change in his voice, and saw fear in his eyes. She said softly, "But you have been deceiving me." There was a stinging film across her eyes. "And—if you're a traitor, so am I."

Discreetly, in her lap, he took her hands.

"You're not a traitor, as you so simplistically put it." He strengthened his grip, against her resentful movement. "If I was trying to feed you guff," he said, "I'd be doing better than this. As it is, all I can do is to swear to you that I haven't asked you, and won't ask you, to do anything against what you believe in. And beg you to trust me for a bit longer without knowing why you should, merely on my word to you."

"A bit longer?"

"I would like to ask you, until you have found the enemy in the lounge. But at least, until you come home on Friday."

She murmured, "I'm afraid of coming—home." Out of the corner of her eye she saw him bow his head.

He whispered, "That's terrible. But I must accept it." She sensed he had turned to look at her. "Will you trust me—that far?"

"I'll stay until Friday. I won't go to the people at Hill House."

"Thank you."

Again that crazy suspicion that somewhere, ruefully, he was smiling.

"I could, you know, just walk out of Hill House and away. It wouldn't really be very difficult."

"It might be more difficult than you think." The second stab of physical fear almost took her breath away. "But you won't do it. What I do suggest," he went on smoothly, and already it was impossible to know if he had really been threatening her, "is that you start having a bit more rest. Stay in your room more."

"I may have to." She told him what had happened in the early part of the night.

"Well, then, take advantage of it, if they lock you in, by trying to sleep."

"You're not really bothered about that, either, are you?"

"God in heaven, I'm bothered all right. And not least for you and your safety and your state of mind."

For the second time there was a convincing passion in his voice, and despite herself she was warmed by it.

"Oh, I don't think I'm really turning into Miss Jones."

"Tell me one thing." All trace of concern had gone, in a few seconds. "Did Tracy—when Tracy knocked the young man for six, as you put it, did she seem—professional?"

She thought it was a strange question. "It was just a hefty kick, really. She had the advantage of taking him unaware from the back. And she told him she'd been through a course in female self-defence." She remembered something else. "She also told him she was going to call the police, but when he escaped through the window she didn't. The only thing she seemed concerned with, then, was clearing up all the evidence. So . . ."

"I see. Thank you." Had he very slightly relaxed? "Is there anything else you feel you can tell me?"

"There is one thing." She had forgotten about Mr. Weston's visit until that moment. There seemed no reason to withhold an account of it. Julian listened in silence but she thought they were sharing a brief amusement. When she had finished he gripped her hand.

"You've come with credit out of every moment of an appalling night. I'm proud of you. Please go on until Friday."

"I've told you I will." With more of the luck she had had in the night, she might complete the job for which she had been hired if she went on pretending to believe in it, thinking on narrow professional lines. And then, when she was less tired and bewildered, she could decide where to pass the information on . . . "And if I still get nowhere?"

"Then you still come home on Friday, and you go back or you don't."

And if she didn't go back, what would she be doing?

If Julian is prepared to kill me, I'm prepared to die.

Helen drew a deep breath, into the sudden clarity.

"I'll do all I promised to do," she said, "until Friday."

"I know you will. Now I think we must remember your tea." He wasn't going to ask her to renew her undertaking not to go to the authorities at Hill House. He, at least, retained his faith. The irony of it made her give a sudden yelp of laughter.

"Here, hold on."

She turned to him, and he was looking at her in alarm. His faith in her was after all no more than the usual qualified faith of men in women.

"Please don't worry." She spoke to the windscreen. "I'm not going to crack up."

"I don't really think you are." His hand was in her lap again. "But I worry about you."

"About what I might do, you're bound to."

Oh, but women could be petty, even when inside they had never been more serious and responsible.

He laced her fingers.

"No, I don't worry about that."

"I'm sorry, I don't really think you do."

"You're very intelligent. What did you *do* when you were Mrs. John Markham?"

If only it was simply he and she, on this sunny day at the seaside!

"Mrs. John Markham entertained a great deal," reported Helen, "kept a beautiful home (it featured once in a glossy magazine), travelled extensively with her executive husband, sat on a few locally important committees, read all the latest biographies, and—resisted a sort of undercurrent of regret."

"Did she acknowledge the regret?"

"I don't think so, quite. But I can't remember very well. She disappeared without trace."

He held her hand tight for a few seconds, and she let him. Neither spoke until his words of cheerful encouragement to his sister as he helped her out of the car at the front door of Hill House. Waiting beside him on the step, Helen felt better for their meeting. And convinced that there was no reason why she should.

2

"Here we are!" The deputy matron was at the front door, her hard blonde hair glinting in the sunlight. "Back in nice time for tea!" In the hall she started to unbutton Miss Jones's coat, pausing with her hands on the lapels. "Did we get our ice-creams, then?"

"We did," reassured Mr. Jones politely.

"Nurse!" Once again Nurse Jackie was summoned as she set foot on the bottom stair. "Just take Miss Jones's coat up with you, will you, dear?" Mrs. Armitage undid the rest of the buttons quickly, pushing the coat back from Helen's shoulders into Nurse Jackie's waiting arms. She turned a brilliant gaze on Julian.

"No point in my suggesting that I should take Miss Jones through into the lounge, is there, Mr. Jones?"

"Thank you, Mrs. Armitage, but I think I should like—"

He broke off, because the front doorbell was ringing so long and uninterrupted a peal, to the accompaniment of frenzied knocking on the centre panel. Mrs. Armitage clicked her tongue and bustled the few steps necessary to open it.

"Well, really . . ." she began, and then recoiled, gazed in

shock, ran forward with her arms out. She staggered back into the hall, supporting a limp body and calling for nurses.

Julian put pressure on Helen's shoulder, and she sat down on the hall settee. The limp body, with Julian's help, was stowed beside her. It was a few seconds before she recognized Mrs. Wellington's sophisticated daughter, and by then Mrs. Winters was struggling to her feet and wildly talking. When she became coherent she had the deputy matron, Mr. Jones, Sister Wendy and Nurse Jackie to listen and support her.

"Perhaps I should have gone to the police," gasped Mrs. Winters. "Or the hospital . . . but I just drove back here. Oh God, perhaps I should have gone to the hospital . . . There were lots of people on the front but I didn't . . . I couldn't . . . I just drove back here. Oh, please, go out and look. I think she's dead. She didn't move. She didn't move all the way home, she wouldn't speak to me. And there's blood. I didn't look, I just found it on my hands when I touched her. Oh God, she can't be dead. Go and *look!*"

Mr. Jones was already through the front door, followed by Sister Wendy. Mrs. Winters went on talking. "I'd only gone off to get her an ice-cream. I was only away a moment. She was sitting just as I'd left her. You know—she sits for ages very quietly with her eyes closed. And she never has any colour. At first I didn't realize . . . And then when she wouldn't take the cornet out of my hand, I touched her, and there was the blood. And she still didn't move and didn't move . . . Perhaps I should have gone to the police . . . or the hospital . . . Oh God, I should have gone to the hospital . . . Oh, please . . ." She burst into hysterical weeping.

"Sit down!" ordered Nurse Jackie. She eased the suddenly unresisting Mrs. Winters back on to the settee. Helen noticed red-brown smears on the white dress as well as the hands. Julian came in and whispered to the deputy matron. She ran across the hall and Helen heard the dialling of the telephone on the staff desk.

"Where is she?" shouted Mrs. Wellington's daughter, struggling to get up again. "Why don't they bring her in?"

"We will bring her in," said Julian gently. He knelt on the

floor beside the settee, and she leaned back under the pressure of his hands on her arms, or the message of his insistent eyes. "You must be brave," he said. "Your mother is dead. No, don't get up just yet." He continued to hold her arms at her sides, to lean over her. "She died right away. There's no doubt about that."

"Right away when? Why? Why did she die at all? I know she had cancer but it doesn't kill you—like that. Or bleed . . . Why did she die? Oh, please . . ."

"Listen," said Julian. "You must know. While you were away from the car, someone stabbed your mother. They stabbed her to the heart, just once, and she died right away."

He put his face against the face of Mrs. Wellington's daughter, slightly muffling the scream. "Don't—don't," murmured Julian, and even if she hadn't loved him Helen would have been unable to believe he was not truly compassionate. "I promise you she knew nothing about it. And Sister Wendy said something to me just now. Listen. *Listen.* Sister Wendy told me that the future for your mother was going to be horrible. She's been spared more and more suffering. There was no real living left for her. You must think of that. You must."

Mrs. Winters nodded her head against the back of the settee. Her eyes were closed and tears cascaded from under her lids. Julian glanced up at Mrs. Armitage, who now stood beside him.

"Who else is there?"

"No one we know of, Mr. Jones."

Mrs. Winters rolled her head from side to side, still without opening her eyes. It was the only time Helen was reminded of the mother.

"There isn't anyone but me."

"Do you think," asked Julian gently, "that you might have seen anyone near the car?"

"When I was coming back with the ice-creams there was a young man. By the window. He cycled away. Oh, please . . ."

Nurse Jackie was whispering to Julian. He nodded and went outside. Nurse Jackie held out her hands to Mrs. Winters.

"Come along, lovey. Have a little lie-down."

Docile, Mrs. Wellington's daughter let herself be helped slowly upstairs. As she disappeared from sight, Sister Wendy and Mr. Jones came in carrying Mrs. Wellington's body under a tartan car-rug.

3

"Poor Miss Jones!" The deputy matron bustled back across the hall and patted Helen's shoulder where she still sat tucked into the corner of the settee. "First Mrs. Barker and now . . . It's just as well the poor darling doesn't know the time of day."

"She can still be frightened," said Mr. Jones, following Mrs. Armitage more slowly from the back of the hall, "if something actually threatens her." A piece of hair had fallen over his forehead, and he looked uncharacteristically disturbed. He pushed the hair back so roughly he left it more untidy. "All right, sweetheart?" He didn't meet her staring eyes.

"All right . . . But Julian, I wish . . ."

She wished she might talk to him. Wished she didn't remember the harsh pressure of Rupert's fingers on her shoulder the last time he had been at Hill House and Mrs. Wellington had said . . . What had she said?

You . . . Miss Jones . . . You're not the fool you look.

Dangerous, it might be thought, to have someone so perceptive sitting so close to the phoney Miss Jones, giving the whole room, at the top of her voice, the benefit of her observations . . .

No, Julian, not that!

She longed not to be telling herself, over and over again in thankfulness, that he had been with her all the time Mrs. Wellington had been out.

"Now, sweetheart, I really think you would be better in the lounge."

"Of course, Mr. Jones, I'm sorry, we should have seen to it that she was taken through. But in all the excitement . . . I don't mean excitement, of course, but it's all been . . ." The deputy matron hovered effusively.

The front doorbell rang again as Julian got Helen to her feet. Showing her annoyance, Mrs. Armitage went to answer it. Two men came into the hall. Helen thought there was something particular about them before she saw them tucking small wallets back inside their jacket pockets.

"I think she's asleep," Mrs. Armitage was saying uncertainly.

"I beg your pardon, madam." The older of the two men advanced so that the deputy matron had to walk backwards to remain in front of him. She bumped into Mr. Weston who, crossing the hall, had cast one glance at the two men and was bolting for the cloakroom.

"Really, Mr. Weston! Asleep . . ." repeated the deputy matron.

"We understood, madam, that the wound was fatal."

"Oh!" Mrs. Armitage's face cleared, and Helen had to cough into her hand, remembering two words in quotation marks on John's grandfather's gravestone. *Only sleeping.* It was rather absurd to feel shocked by her reaction, in view of all that was happening.

"I'm sorry," said Mrs. Armitage to the two men. "Yes, I'm afraid Mrs. Wellington's wound was certainly fatal. I was speaking of her daughter, Mrs. Winters, who is resting upstairs—"

"We'll have a look at the body first, if you please. A pity it was moved."

"That was at my suggestion." Mr. Jones had stepped forward. "I'm sorry, Officer. I was thinking of the effect on visitors. And, indeed, on those who live—"

"You are, sir?"

"Merely a visitor myself." Julian smiled apologetically, and the senior policeman, shaking his head, turned back to the deputy matron.

"If you will just show me."

"Of course, Officer."

Mrs. Armitage and the two policemen set off for the kitchen, and Helen regretted having suppressed her inclination, during the time they had abandoned Miss Jones, to go to the kitchen herself. Julian took her arm and they walked into the lounge.

There all was undisturbed apathy. Of the men, only Mr. Thomas was present, dozing in his corner. Even Miss Duncan was neatly asleep, her large book open on her knees.

A cough sounded behind them as they paused in the doorway. "Excuse me," said Mr. Weston, in his husky little voice, "I was thinking it must be tea-time."

He coughed again. Despite his attempt at jocularity the hand which he put up to his tie was trembling. Helen saw him glance at Mrs. Wellington's empty chair, but he could have noticed that she always reacted in some way when he cleared his throat.

"I think tea will be a little late today," murmured Julian. "Mrs. Wellington has had an accident."

"Mrs. Wellington . . ." Mr. Weston broke off to cough again. He kept glancing towards the door.

"Have you been out this afternoon, Mr. Weston?" queried Julian politely.

"Eh?" Mr. Weston made a visible effort of bringing his mind to bear on what Mr. Jones was saying. "This afternoon? Out? No. Spent the afternoon in m'room reading. Mrs. Wellington had an accident, you say? Is that why the police . . . I mean . . ." Mr. Weston's forehead gleamed with sweat, he smiled beseechingly at Julian.

"I believe so. Now, sweetheart." Mr. Jones guided his sister to her seat and helped her to arrange herself. Mr. Weston sat on the edge of a vacant chair.

"I'll leave you now, Helen." He leaned down and lightly kissed the corner of her mouth. She shuddered as he straightened up, and for a few seconds he looked her searchingly in the eyes.

"Julian . . . Come soon . . ."

"I will, darling, I will. Have a good tea, now."

She was the last to be taken into the dining-room. As she walked across the lounge, encouraged by Nurse Hazel, she could hear Mrs. Wayne-Jenkins's loud indignant voice coming from the hall. With the loss of both Mrs. Barker and Mrs.

Wellington, Mr. Thomas was now alone at a table with Mrs. Charlesworth, and aware of it.

"Mrs. Wellington out to tea, then?" he kept asking brightly, of Mrs. Charlesworth's unresponsive face.

"Yes," said Nurse Hazel at last in a muffled voice, bending down to pick up a wiggle of spaghetti Miss Jones had let fall from her fork on to the floor. "Now, Miss Jones, let's sit properly at the table, shall we?"

"Sit properly, yes."

Mrs. Wellington's daughter might just have wanted to spare her mother her final agonies, and to spare herself the consequences of what she saw as an act of mercy.

"That's better. But you're not getting on very well, are you? Look, Mrs. Anthony's nearly finished!"

"Getting on . . ."

But Mrs. Winters would never have done it *that* way. And The Laurels would probably not have been able to do it any other.

CHAPTER 13

1

"How did she get in, Mrs. Armitage?" asked Matron icily.

The deputy matron spread helpless hands. "She just—*came* in, Matron. On her way to complain to Mrs. Roberts about something, of course, and she just—came in. And it was the moment when the police were looking at—at the body, and so of course she—Mrs. Wayne-Jenkins—saw it too and—I agree it was all most unfortunate."

"I can think of stronger words, Mrs. Armitage. I can think of gross negligence, for a start. An elementary gesture, I should have thought, to secure the door. However, the damage is done, and no doubt will be compounded in due course in the newspapers."

"Mrs. Wayne-Jenkins has no idea," said the deputy matron in flustered eagerness, "how Mrs. Wellington died."

"At the moment, I should hope not." The cold glance fell on Helen, sitting in the kitchen armchair. "But Mrs. Wayne-Jenkins is not, I am afraid, like Miss Jones. She will spread the news all over the house, and in the most inflammatory way."

"I'm afraid she's in the lounge at the moment, Matron."

Helen, who until that moment had been congratulating herself on again being present at a kitchen encounter between the matron and the deputy matron, had to force herself to get to her feet slowly, slowly to drift towards the kitchen door. Already, anyway, she had missed the immediate reactions.

Mrs. Wayne-Jenkins was still in the lounge, standing in front of Mr. Thomas, who was leaning forward in his chair with the air of a man doing what he could.

"She's dead, Mr. Thomas," Mrs. Wayne-Jenkins was saying, loudly and impatiently. "*Dead.*"

Mr. Thomas scratched his head in perplexity. His was a world, now, in which such large concepts had no place.

"Mrs. Wellington went out to tea," he offered hopefully, his face brightening again towards its normal cheerfulness. "Her daughter came for her."

"*Oh!*" Mrs. Wayne-Jenkins swung petulantly away from him. She stood by the door, looking fiercely round the room. "Mrs. Wellington's dead," she repeated aggressively. "Lying on the kitchen table. *Yes!*" Although no one had ventured to contradict her. "I went in to tell Mrs. Roberts about that last batch of rock cakes. Rock cakes, indeed! And Mrs. Wellington was lying on the kitchen table. Two strange men peering at her. It's a disgrace."

"I entirely agree with you," snapped Miss Duncan. Mrs. Wayne-Jenkins glared at her, no doubt preferring hostility to agreement, particularly as regarded her only remaining rival.

But there appeared to be no alternative response: Miss Protheroe was looking down at her lap, Mrs. Anthony smiling her unruffled smile, Miss Welch and Mrs. Charlesworth staring, Mrs. Stoddart fiddling with the arm of her chair and softly muttering. Mr. Thomas had hidden himself behind his newspaper.

Mrs. Wayne-Jenkins flounced round, nearly knocking Helen over.

"And you, you fool!"

Leaning against the doorpost, Helen saw the encounter in the hall with Mr. Corlett and heard the beginnings of the duet between Mrs. Wayne-Jenkins's strident contralto and his soothing tenor.

"What a barbarian!"

Miss Duncan banged her book shut, then opened it and began to search for her page. To Helen's surprise Miss Protheroe was at her elbow, plucking gently at her sleeve and helping her to her chair.

"Never mind, dear," said Miss Protheroe to Miss Duncan, as they went past. "I expect she had a shock."

"We all have shocks." Miss Duncan slapped the open pages of her book.

"Well, it must have been quite a big one," said Miss Protheroe mildly, as Helen sank into her seat.

"The woman's an idiot. She must be exaggerating."

"I don't see how you could exaggerate a thing like that. I mean, Mrs. Wellington was either dead on the kitchen table—oh dear!—or she wasn't. And the two men were either there or they weren't. I think it must be true, Miss Duncan."

"We'll know soon enough."

"Oh dear, yes, we will."

Miss Protheroe tripped back to her place and Miss Duncan bent her head over her reading. When Matron came in a few moments later, all was its usual immobility and silence. She crossed the room and switched on the television. Gales of laughter heralded the image. It was the beginning of an old and lengthy comedy feature film, for which Helen was grateful.

Horlicks and a biscuit arrived half way through it and at the end, before there was time to start thinking, Nurse Jackie was there to take her up to bed.

Nurse Jackie was even more blotched and rosy than usual and, Helen thought, even more gentle and protective towards her frail charges.

"Nice girl," said Helen on the stairs. They were half way up when they heard the flying feet. Nurse Hazel was on the landing above them.

"Jackie, for heaven's sake!"

"What is it?" Nurse Jackie went on steadily climbing with Miss Jones.

"It's Mrs. Harvey. She's gone and died!"

"Mrs. Harvey?"

"Just lying there. Dead. Now, of all times!"

"Now, of all times!"

The words were repeated from behind Nurse Hazel, in an unfamiliar high-pitched voice, and were followed by a dreadful snicker of laughter. The deputy matron stumbled into sight, her laughter mounting in pitch and volume.

"Better go and tell Mrs. Wayne-Jenkins!" shrieked the deputy matron. Nurse Hazel turned and slapped her sharply across the face and she slumped against the wall, her laughter dwindling into hiccups as she billowed slowly to the floor, her skirt rising round her as if she was inflated.

"She's all right now," said Nurse Hazel, bending over her. "Gosh, though."

"Mrs. Harvey . . ."

"We can't do anything. Will you get Matron? Or Sister Wendy."

"Yes. Just let me put Miss Jones in. Thank heaven she can see to herself."

In Helen's last view of the deputy matron she was sitting against the wall with her fat legs out in front of her, silently sobbing. The sound of tears, now, came from the open door of the room for two, heart-rendingly.

"I'll see you later, darling," said Nurse Jackie to Miss Jones, at her bedroom door. Helen heard the key turn in the lock.

2

It was more likely that Nurse Jackie had decided they could do, in the extraordinary circumstances, without Miss Jones hanging around, than that a policy had been decided upon, and implemented. And there was a sense almost of relief in her enforced inactivity. She undressed in Miss Jones's usual slow steady way, still hearing a confusion of voices from the landing which she welcomed for drowning the unhappiness of Mrs. Lambert. When she was ready she got into bed and lay down, realizing that a physical tension had left her and that her body at least was relaxed. With her head turned on the pillow she could see an orange lake in the lower sky, one star in the featureless grey expanse above it. Its real beauty was in its remoteness from her troubled present and unthinkable future . . .

Mrs. Harvey must have died because she could no longer suffer the awful truncation of her body. Julian couldn't have had anything to do with that . . .

She mustn't think about Julian, because then she would think about being with him, about loving him, about giving and being given, and that made the other thoughts so much worse . . .

Did a bad present stain back over a good past, destroying it in retrospect? She should know, if anyone did, because of what had happened with John. Yet, thinking about that, it didn't help her. The memories of what at the time had seemed to be good were no longer so, certainly, but that wasn't because of what John had done, it was because she knew, now, something so much better.

It was no good. Mrs. Wellington, Mrs. Harvey, the deputy matron, Mrs. Wayne-Jenkins, the young man and the Hill House letterhead, nothing and no one could she interpose between herself and the knowledge of the miraculous existence of one man.

At least, as she struggled against the tears which as Miss

Jones she must never shed, her exhaustion eventually put her to dreamless sleep.

She hadn't set her inner alarm, but when she awoke she knew before she looked at the clock that it was half past six, and time to start thinking again, constructively. She must have started the process during sleep, because she awoke with the knowledge that observation could no longer be enough, that if she wanted to complete her assignment she must lay individual siege to each and every inmate of Hill House. She must exaggerate either Miss Jones's curiosity or her proneness to agitation, both of which qualities would enable her, in character, to reach out in admiration or for support, and to touch suddenly, sharply . . . Julian's team at The Laurels had taught her that there were areas of particular sensitivity. And then, perhaps, if she touched the right person, that person, unsuspicious of the feeble society by which he or she was surrounded, might vent the frustration of the masquerade in an uncharacteristic retaliation . . . Miss Protheroe for a vital second ungentle, Mr. Thomas no longer vague, Mr. Corlett uncourteous, Miss Welch and Mrs. Charlesworth focusing their eyes, Mrs. Anthony unsmiling, Mrs. Wayne-Jenkins suddenly small-scaled, Mr. Weston concentrated, Miss Duncan—Miss Duncan would be difficult.

And so would they all. And Helen Markham, attacked violently and without warning from behind, had not given herself away.

Nevertheless, on a horrible instant of mingled weariness and resolve, she knew she must make the effort.

She would just lie in bed a bit longer, watching the sun rise in a pale calm sky and thinking there were two and a half days left before Julian came to take her home and . . . Anyway, the bedroom door could well be locked until someone came in with her breakfast. She hadn't the energy or the interest to get up and try it . . .

"Well, Miss Jones, dear, I've always wondered why you didn't let me give you your breakfast in bed. Now, isn't this nice? I'll just bring your table over and it'll be so comfy and easy."

Nurse Jackie's face was lop-sided with weeping, her smile especially affectionate.

After breakfast Helen got up and dressed and wandered out on to the landing, in reluctant pursuit of a solitary Hill House patient. Mrs. Wayne-Jenkins's door was locked, and Mrs. Lambert's she wouldn't yet open. The men's room contained the three men, and the only people who came into the cloakroom were accompanied by a nurse. It was a further self-indulgence to go into the kitchen, but her heart was pounding so heavily she thought she might faint. The kitchen table was covered with mixing bowls and cooking implements. Mrs. Roberts smiled at Miss Jones over her pastry. As Helen installed herself in the armchair Tracy came out of the still-room with some bottles of milk which she plonked down.

"What about Mrs. Harvey, then?" said Tracy.

"Heart gave out," responded Mrs. Roberts shortly. "Who could be sorry?"

"I know, Mrs. Roberts, I wasn't . . ." Tracy was back in her accustomed position at the sink. "I gather that poor Mrs. Winters got a grilling."

"You shouldn't gossip with Sandra and Jackie." Mrs. Roberts increased the vigour of her elbow. "Mrs. Winters knew what her mother had to expect. They think she might have wanted to spare her."

"Like that?" Tracy turned round to pose the question.

"It's not likely, I'll agree."

"How's Mrs. Armitage this morning?"

"All right, I gather. Matron's ordered her to stay in bed today and I think she'll go away for a bit of a rest. Hurry up with those pots, Tracy O'Connor."

Helen got slowly to her feet. The panic had subsided, and the kitchen was a refuge now, rather than an arena. She should be back in action.

"All right, then, lovey?" Mrs. Roberts was watching her as she crossed the floor. Also Tracy, less openly.

"All right. Just going . . . Think I should . . ."

"You do," said Mrs. Roberts.

In the lounge Mr. Thomas was reading his paper, and Miss

Duncan her book. The seating had been subtly rearranged so that the two chairs occupied by Mrs. Stoddart and Miss Duncan now obliterated the erstwhile site of Mrs. Wellington's.

"Hello, dear," said Mrs. Anthony as Helen sat down. "I hope Mary will come today." She had a wistful look which Helen found touching.

Mrs. Anthony patted her hand. She could have covered Mrs. Anthony's hand with her own free hand, pressed, squeezed . . . But Miss Duncan was staring at her. It would have to be luck, and luck could, she thought wearily, be prompted. She got to her feet again and went across the hall into the cloakroom, where she sat down on the cork seat.

Nurse Jackie with Mrs. Stoddart. Nurse Jackie with Miss Welch. It was weak and craven, to be praying continuously that it wouldn't be a man. Miss Protheroe. Very briefly in one of the lavatories, then washing her small rough hands. Holding one of them out to Miss Jones, who got to her feet and came close.

Miss Protheroe was wearing a pendant shaped like a star. A birthday present from her nephew, as Sister Wendy, rather than Miss Protheroe, had told them all.

"Nice . . ." Helen put her hand out, held the light, gold-coloured thing, couldn't violate the thin chest behind it, couldn't . . . Her hand travelled up the cheap chain, to the neck, Miss Jones murmured, Helen's fingers pressed . . .

Miss Protheroe's hand was on Miss Jones's wrist, edging it firmly but gently away. She had winced, yes, had caught her breath, but the pale blue eyes hadn't changed, they were just looking a little troubled and sad. If Miss Protheroe was as good an actress as Helen Markham, what had Helen achieved but a renewed vigilance, and perhaps a death warrant signed in a different place?

"Nice . . . Mustn't touch. Sorry." Miss Jones fluttered a hand in the air and Miss Protheroe, the woman Helen would like to think of as dear, good Miss Protheroe, caught it and held it.

"Time for lunch," said Miss Protheroe. She held Miss Jones's hand across the hall and all the way to their table.

3

Lunch, where she was not hungry but, seeing or imagining an additional scrutiny by Miss Protheroe, must eventually empty her plate. People settling back into their chairs, their faces towards the screen, their eyes for the most part beyond or short of it. A few somnolent moments, then the visiting beginning. Miss Welch's sister. Sitting down beside Miss Welch, explaining why she wasn't taking her out today. Mrs. Stoddart's sister. Miss Protheroe's niece, beginning at once to slough off her complaints of the week on to that silent reactionless little figure. Miss Anthony. Sitting down in her usual position close to her mother, the vague smile towards Miss Jones.

"I'm glad to see you, darling." Mrs. Anthony rather faintly, but smiling now. "I missed you yesterday." There was a slight colour in one of Miss Anthony's pale cheeks. "They said you weren't well."

"It was only a headache, Mother, it's gone now. I lay down in the afternoon."

"So long as you're all right now, dear. Give me your hand."

Miss Anthony held her left hand out towards her mother, and it was as if Helen was watching the television because Miss Anthony dissolved, in her place there was a young man, left arm raised, a bright red line breaking out on the back of the hand from fingernail to wrist, then blurring. The only difference, as the picture dissolved back again, was that the red line was sharp, dark . . . No, there were other differences, of course, there was no moustache, there was more hair on the head, there was a red mark on the cheek. But that wasn't really a difference, because the cheek had fallen against a table.

The figure, the voice, she had known them and not known them. *And Mrs. Wellington had said something else.*

She had a photographic memory, she had only to turn back to the place where she had found Mrs. Wellington's remark about Miss Jones, and read it more carefully. Yes, there it was. Mrs. Wellington, leaning forward, furiously angry. Turning her gaze on Miss Jones from Mrs. Anthony. *Having already said "You're not the fool you look."*

So someone as well as Rupert had had a motive to be on the safe side . . . *I lay down in the afternoon.* And the young man cycled beside the sea.

The Anthonys had been so concerned with what Mrs. Wellington had said about the mother, they might not have noticed what came next. *You're not, either.* But the daughter had already been satisfied. Mary had had her little lamb . . . Her sense of relief wasn't all because the young man had not come a third time, part of it was because she knew there was one dreadful thing which Julian hadn't done . . .

With an effort as great as any she had made since coming to Hill House, Helen went on staring just past Miss Anthony.

"Poor Mary."

"Really, Mother, I'm all right now."

Miss Anthony was gazing round the room in her usual apparently unseeing way. Oh, but the pale creature had panache as well as venom! And the confidence that everyone *was* the fool he or she looked . . .

Helen's moment of self-congratulation was short-lived, thoughts and hindsights were tumbling in her head like a snowstorm. Mrs. Anthony, about whom there had probably been less to observe and record than about anyone else. The chameleon girl, who looked like no one and everyone. No wonder she was giddy. Going from utter ignorance to utter understanding in the space of a second . . .

She would have no qualm of conscience in telling Julian about the Anthonys—if she didn't make herself assume his ignorance she couldn't make herself do anything else—because Miss Anthony was a sadist whatever her allegiance, and couldn't be exposed in too many places. If it didn't seem that Miss Anthony would suffer through exposure to Julian. Helen could offer her up to Hill House. If she got the chance . . .

"It's a nice day, Mother, I think we should go for a little run."

Yes, of course Miss Anthony would think that. And she,

Helen, thought that the next forty-eight hours would be the longest of her life. Whatever the complications of the Anthonys and Julian and the two houses, her own job was done. They would have to sort it out now, and let her rest. Julian might be devising a long rest . . .

Meanwhile, she could only sit and stare. Or run away? The door was locked but she could get someone else's clothes by sleight or violence (how her confidence had grown), and then be Miss Jones's sane sister long enough for the door to be opened and . . .

"*It might be more difficult than you think.*"

But it wasn't so much the threat, as the promise . . . Julian.

She would not have believed it possible to long for, and to dread, the same thing.

And alternate dreams of love and escape would at least help to pass the time . . .

The Anthonys were on their way to the door. She couldn't look after them, but she heard Miss Anthony say, in her soft expressionless girl's voice, "I'm so sorry. Be careful, Mother," and then a shuffle of feet.

"That's all right."

A familiar voice, but an unexpected one. Helen turned her head enough to see the tall blonde girl advancing with a visitor's chair dangling from her hand.

"Hello, Auntie."

Cora set the chair down opposite Helen and plumped into it, leaning forward to take Helen's hand. "How are you, then?"

"I'm very well. How nice. Dear, I don't know . . ."

Cora was looking at her keenly if covertly.

"I thought it was time I paid you a visit, Auntie."

"Very nice," commented Miss Jones.

Even if it meant breaking her rule, Cora must not be allowed to depart without her. She could go to the loo, and, if Cora didn't accompany her, stay there until she followed. She could go upstairs and do the same thing. Or—she could do what she did with Julian. He and she had never put it into words between them, that for her to press his palm was her signal she wanted to talk, but he might have codified it for Cora.

"Ice-cream!" announced Miss Jones, pressing her fingers into her niece's palm.

"Well, now," responded Cora smoothly. "You still know what you like, Auntie, don't you? I was just going to suggest having a little run, it's such a nice day. So we'll get some ice-cream as well."

"Good girl. Very nice. You have ice-cream."

"Oh, I shall, you shan't have it all to yourself. Up you get, now."

She leaned on Cora's cool strong wrist as they went slowly out to the hall. Cora put her on the hall settee, rang the bell, bounded up the stairs two at a time, and came down again with Miss Jones's coat just as Nurse Jackie arrived to open the front door.

"I'm sorry to hear . . ." Cora said to Nurse Jackie.

"Thanks." Nurse Jackie was still puffy-eyed. "And Mrs. Harvey died last night."

"Mrs. Harvey?"

"You probably never saw her, Miss Jones. She never came down. She'd lost both her legs."

Cora appeared to wince at this revelation. "It could only be as well, then."

"Oh, I know. But it's her sister. Simple-minded."

"I'm sorry."

Cora hid her impatience well. Nurse Jackie smiled wanly and opened the door for them. Competently, Cora helped Helen into the car and they started off.

As they paused between the gateposts Helen said softly, "The Laurels, please, Cora."

Cora said as quietly, not moving her head, "There's not enough time. You can talk at the pier."

"Not today. I've finished my job. I've discovered all Julian wants to know and he must be told. We must go back."

The word "home" had stuck in her throat.

"Very well."

"Thanks for responding. And for coming, of course. Why did you come?"

"Julian suggested I had a look at you." Warmth and cold gushed together, making her giddy again. "Want to say anything now?"

"Is Julian in?"

"He is."

"I think I'll hold it."

"Probably best."

They didn't speak again until they pulled up at the front door of The Laurels.

"You'd better wait, Auntie," said Cora then. "And let me help you out."

She dropped Helen's arm as the front door clicked to behind them.

"He's in the office."

"Thank you." She went across the hall and knocked on the office door, opening it without waiting for a response.

He glanced up from behind his desk, the look of impatience turning to what she could only see as anxiety.

"Helen, for God's sake!"

He was on his feet, coming round the desk.

"It's all right," she said, going to meet him. Their hands clasped. "I got Cora to bring me home because I've finished my job. I know now who the enemy is."

"Know for certain?"

"Yes." But not everything for certain, thank God not everything.

"Sit down."

He dropped her hands and she realized she had talked about coming home. Giddiness overcame her again, and it seemed a long way away that he was wrenching the door open, calling to Cora.

Cora was there at once.

"Ring up Hill House, will you," said Julian, "and tell them you felt Auntie was a bit under the weather and so we've decided to let her spend the night at home."

CHAPTER 14

1

"I thought you would refuse to tell me."

"I don't expect I shall tell you. I expect you know it already."

"We can only work on the assumption that I don't."

"Yes. Yes. And anyway, I don't mind telling you. Because it involves your young man, to whom I don't exactly owe any loyalty."

"The young man?"

It was there again, that instant one hundred per cent concentration.

She said indifferently, "The young man is Miss Anthony."

"I don't understand you."

The amazement was perfectly done, but the leap of her heart was so faint she told her whole story in the same dull, dreary way.

"Miss Anthony is the female of the species," she said finally. "I'm sure of that, too. Wears a wig when she visits the old lady. Wears a moustache when she marauds. Slim boyish figure."

"The look of the hand had somehow gone into my mind intact, and it was exactly reproduced, given the time to harden the line of the wound. And the cheek bruise was just where he/she fell against the kitchen table. And I've no doubt at all that Mrs. Wellington said Mrs. Anthony as well as Miss Jones wasn't the fool she looked—Rupert heard it too, so you can check. And when you think about it—Mrs. Anthony is the patient who's declared herself least. I mean, one could think anything one wanted about Mrs. Anthony."

"No distinguishing features."

"None. Like Miss Anthony. No eccentric persona to keep up. I remember thinking Miss Welch must be innocent, no one could go on staring like that, day in and day out, looking so freshly terrified all the time. I should have gone the logical step on, and tried to think who had the easiest part. Well, I did in a way, but I inclined to Miss Protheroe."

"You thought the young man was familiar."

"That never stopped teasing me. Even the voice." There really wasn't anything more to say on the only subject which had been between her and the subject of the future. "So—I've finished." *Am finished?* She sat very still, her hands in her lap, strangely relaxed, unaware of that body which so soon might be suffering, or oblivious.

"Not quite. You have an important part still to play. But not tonight, so you will stay here. No need for unnecessary risks. For you or for us." He smiled at her, but his choice of pronouns had made her feel coldly isolated.

"Yes?"

"We'll whizz you back after lunch the first day we know Miss Anthony is a-visiting."

She murmured, "You have ways of finding out."

"We have. You'll take your place in the usual way, and just after Miss Anthony leaves I'll press your hand and you'll lean across to Mrs. Anthony and tell her the game's up."

"In so many words?"

"Why not in so many words? Why not be a bit swash-buckling? It doesn't all that much matter what words you use, anyway, the medium will be the message."

"And what do I do then?"

"Then, my dear, you remain quietly seated. You let things go on exactly as usual. Unless . . ." He paused, looking down at his desk. Through the net curtain she could see a crow edging crabwise across the lawn towards the window. "Unless an aggressive move is made against you. Then Helen Markham will defend herself."

"An aggressive move is likely?"

"It's possible." They gazed at one another. It was as if she had always known this moment would arrive. "Once we've left you, don't go anywhere alone, or at anyone's invitation. Join another patient on a trip to the cloakroom. Until bedtime. When bedtime comes let yourself be taken up in the normal way. Get into bed. But don't go to sleep. No!"—as despite herself she half rose from her chair—"There will be protection, but it's best not to be taken unawares . . . And best not to fight your own battle, once you're in bed."

"No Miss Anthony." At least she would be spared those granite-grey eyes.

"Miss Anthony, I promise you, will not get very far."

"And if she doesn't show up tomorrow, we postpone the play until she does?"

"Yes."

"I hope it can be—finished—tomorrow." And she was glad there was the possibility that an end might come at Hill House rather than The Laurels. Abroad, rather than at home.

"You can rest until then."

"I can go through the motions."

As he always did, he had continued to regard her while they talked, but that had been so as not to miss any nuance of her usefulness. Now, he was studying her face because it was hers, Helen's. *But who is Helen, what is she?*

"Helen . . ." His hand moved towards her, but then dropped to his pen, which he picked up to begin doodling on the paper in front of him. She thought suddenly of the night. It was extraordinary how anticipations both joyous and fearful went on surging together. She got to her feet.

"I'll go and change."

He too rose, came round the desk.

"Of course." He could have been ever so slightly at a loss, but so little of his feeling showed in his face. She wondered, not for the first time, whether this was the result of his training, or whether he had started work with a natural advantage.

He glanced at his watch.

"It's four o'clock. Go upstairs and I'll send Mrs. Gray after you with some tea. And a biscuit rather than baked beans and sausage. Stay there until dinner. Or rather, I hope you'll come down half an hour or so before dinner, and have a drink."

"Half an hour," said Helen. "It can mean the justification, for you, of all these weeks. Or relaxing over a drink before dinner."

"As you say." She thought he sighed as he walked to the door. "Dinner at eight, I believe, tonight. I'll be glad if you're down by half past seven."

Because it would show she was still prepared to drink with him, or that she was obedient?

He held the door for her, stood aside so that there was no possibility of her touching him with so much as a fold of her skirt as she went through, immediately closed the door behind her.

The hall was silent and deserted. A thin shaft of sunlight lay across the carpet, in the place where she had noticed it before in the world which now seemed so uncomplicated and far away. She trailed slowly upstairs, into the room she had shared with Julian. It was tidy, her own few pieces still about as she had placed them, a small vase of primroses on the dressing-table. She took her dress off but still felt feeble and slow, it was an effort even to move about the room.

She was suddenly so tired she had to slouch across bathroom and bedroom and on to the bed. Her nightie was under her pillow and she shrugged into it and crawled between the sheets almost in one movement. Mrs. Gray knocked and came in with a tray of tea and biscuits. She put it down beside the bed and considered Helen for a moment.

"I'll pour out for you, Mrs. Markham." She did so in silence.

"Thank you, Mrs. Gray."

It was a macabre but by no means absurd thought, that Mrs. Gray was as likely as any of them to be preparing herself, and a situation, for the disposal of a dangerous agent whose work was almost completed . . .

She would not think like that. She had disciplined herself to so much, she could discipline herself to this. And she was still sure she would want to accept whatever Julian devised for her.

She drank two cups of tea and ate two biscuits, propped up comfortably on her pillows and gazing round the agreeable room. Then she lay down on her side and had time only to register her relaxation before falling into a dreamless sleep.

2

She woke abruptly but without fear, rolling slowly over to see that the clock by the bed said seven. She had the feeling her attention had been attracted in some way, perhaps by a tap on the door to give her the opportunity to be downstairs at half past, as Julian wished. She knew at once that two and a half hours' sleep had been enough to refresh her and give her back the stiffening of will to avoid thoughts of anything but the immediate moment.

She jumped out of bed and ran into the bathroom, finding herself free of Miss Jones. She had a long bath, aware of her health and strength and refusing to feel ironic about them. She put on her favourite dress, rather than Julian's. When she was ready the face in the mirror was radiantly lovely, and she stared at it in surprise before running lightly downstairs and into the drawing-room.

From her pang of disappointment she realized she had been hoping to find Julian alone. In the room with him were Cora and Rupert. They chorused a greeting and she tried, with painful success, to see them as she had seen them the last time they had formed a dinner-party. It was hard to believe the memory was only three nights old.

She was attracting more attention now than she had done then.

"Well done," said Cora.

"I always knew she was clever," said Rupert.

There was an enormous laugh swelling up inside her which she had to choke down. Fortunately she was distracted by the discovery that she was more interested, tonight, in her possible beauty than her brains. It was an unfamiliar exhilaration to know how well she looked, and to see reaction to it on the part of each of them.

"Champagne next time," said Julian, handing her her usual choice of dry sherry, not veiling his admiration.

Cora said, patting the space of sofa beside her, "I don't know how you can manage to look like that."

"Like what?" Helen took the offered place, confident of Cora's explanation.

"Simply—so pretty. One would have expected strain, Auntie rubbing off, as it were."

"There is strain." Julian hadn't moved away after giving her her drink. "I think that's why she looks so beautiful." Oh, but she was glad, whatever he must do with her, however long she had to enjoy the memory, that he had found her beautiful. He put his hand under her chin and turned her face up towards him.

It was an agreeable meal—the food, the wine, the company— and she was aware of a release from tension in the knowledge that she had completed the task which had seemed by turns impossible or non-existent. She was also aware, more fiercely and straightforwardly than she had ever known the sensation, of desire for her lover.

The desire was so strong she grew bored with the conversation over coffee, even though the prospect of tomorrow's final act sharpened its lazy edge. The evening ended when Julian was interrupted in a funny story by a call to the telephone. He came back to them cool and businesslike.

"I think we should go to bed." He was looking at Helen. "We're forgetting we haven't finished."

"Yes, of course." Anxiety fanned her flame.

The two women went up first, said good night on the landing without lingering.

Mrs. Gray had drawn the curtains and turned back the bedspread. Helen undressed and washed quickly, got into bed and lay down, hugging herself against a fit of shivering. Since her investigation of Mrs. Roberts's overall pocket she had thought about this night all the time somewhere underneath her other thoughts, wondering how she should conduct herself. Now it had arrived, and there had been no need to wonder. There was only one possible way.

If he came to her.

The wave of desolation was so strong that for a moment she was nearly choking, burrowing into the bed to escape the cold force. She lay as if paralysed, not sure whether or not she was praying, until she heard the door open, and even then she only gradually relaxed.

She saw his outline turn from black to grey as he took off his dressing-gown. He got into bed and lay down, not touching her. Something in his instant stillness made her arrest her eager movement towards him.

He said quietly, "You're not asleep."

"No."

Her hands were clasped together under her chin, in the attitude she had adopted as a child when she knelt down beside her bed at night.

"Good night, then. Don't worry. About tomorrow—or any other time."

She had no voice, she could only whisper. "Good night."

Hope ebbed more quickly than desire. Eventually, with an economy of movement, he turned on his side away from her, and a few minutes later, being careful not to touch him, she turned on her side towards him, because it was the side on which she always eventually slept.

She lay hurt and indignant, trying to believe he must be suffering as she was, but he breathed so softly and regularly so like the way Mrs. Anthony breathed in the night at Hill House —and she really knew him so little. He could be respecting her principles as she would have failed to respect them herself. And he would of course, whatever his inclinations, have come to lie beside her tonight as simply the most economical and effective means of imprisonment.

3

When she awoke he had gone, and Mrs. Gray was crossing the room with her breakfast tray. She set it down and drew the curtains. The half of the bed where Julian had slept was so neat it reinforced her sense of having spent the night alone.

"Take your time this morning," said Mrs. Gray.

Despite the long sleep Helen's head ached and she still felt tired, the blue of the sky above the net curtain was too bright for her eyes. A vital role to play that afternoon, but no more initiatives. Unless she tried to escape from The Laurels, which would seem to be a more open prison than Hill House. But she wasn't going to try. Whether from love, loyalty, hope or defeatism, she didn't know.

Somehow, as she sat in bed slowly eating toast, nothing seemed worth worrying about, nothing really seemed important. She spent an hour reading the newspaper on her tray, and each item as she came to it seemed more real and absorbing than her own situation. No one disturbed her, although when she came out of the bathroom the tray had gone. It was eleven o'clock by the time she was dressed, herself (*myself?*) but with Miss Jones's clothes set out ready to put on.

Cora was reading another newspaper in the drawing-room, another tray beside her.

"Hello. Coffee?"

"I might as well. Thanks."

She sat heavily down opposite Cora, still feeling tired, aware of the sensation familiar from hotel lounges, when the weather prevents one from going out, or other people whom one is bound to accommodate are tiresome by not being ready or able to make up their minds. Somewhere, she was displeased with the perverseness and triviality of her reactions.

"Are you involved this afternoon?" she asked Cora, as they leaned towards each other to exchange the coffee-cup.

"Not this afternoon." Cora sat back, looking at Helen. "I hear things have upset you."

Helen found herself shrugging. "If I think about it. At the moment I'm not doing."

Cora crossed her long slim legs. "That's wise."

"It isn't so much wise. It's just happened." Even putting her lackadaisical mood into words, it held up. "I'll be keyed up for the job, of course, this afternoon, but otherwise . . ."

"You don't need to be upset. By the way, Father wondered if you'd go and see him in the office when you're ready. That means when you've finished your coffee, of course."

Cora smiled at her. What would Cora do if she suddenly got up and went out through the french window and round the side of the house and across the front garden and out of the gate? She was more interested in the thought of what Cora would do than in the prospect of escape.

Her body felt like lead, and she moved heavily across the hall. Julian smiled at her from behind his desk.

"How are you this morning?"

"I'm all right, thank you."

"Your role now is simple, considering what you've done so far."

"I know. I'm not worrying. Beyond my professional tension, that is."

"Good."

But he had looked at her sharply, and she wished she could sound less cool. He might think she was angry or disappointed, which she no longer was.

"Lunch at twelve-thirty, quickly, and then get ready."

"Yes."

It occurred to her that what she would most like to do was to spend the rest of the day in an armchair, reading *Middlemarch*.

"And . . . please trust me."

"I should like to."

But she could muster hardly any feelings on the subject.

Lunch was cold meat and salad set out for them to help themselves, so that it wasn't glaringly obvious how little everyone ate. They drank water, then coffee, Julian and Rupert and

Cora and Helen. Helen went upstairs afterwards unprompted and dressed up as Miss Jones. She didn't go through the inner process to alter her face, but already it bore little resemblance to the face of the night before. *Who is Helen, what is she?* When she was nearly ready Cora came in and sat down on the bedroom chair. Another jailer? wondered Helen, unconcerned. Cora suggested they should wait in the bedroom until they knew whether the action was on.

The reminder that the end of things might not be reached that day gave her what felt like her strongest emotion for a long time. When the telephone rang she stayed in the room while Cora went out to investigate, wanting something again, but only that she might not have to spend another twenty-four hours in limbo.

"Countdown's begun," said Cora in the doorway.

All at once her heart was as noisy as it was in the early mornings at Hill House.

Downstairs, Julian and Rupert escorted her in silence into the car. Rupert in the back reinforced her sense of imprisonment. They were almost at Hill House before Julian broke the silence.

"The Anthonys have gone out. But that won't affect anything. Whatever you see, whatever you hear, sit in your chair in your usual way when you've done your bit. Go to the cloakroom with at least two other people, and defend yourself if necessary. Don't accept any invitations, except to go up to bed. Once in your bedroom, revert entirely to Miss Jones. Nothing may happen. But if it does, there will be protection. Thank you for going back."

She murmured, "Was there a choice?"

"Thank you for going back unprotestingly. Good luck, Helen."

The wheels scrunched on Hill House's luxuriant gravel. Sister Wendy was there to let them in.

"Miss Jones, then! And two escorts, what a lucky girl! All right now, lovey?"

"All right. Thank you . . ."

"My nephew and I are going on up to London," said Julian.

"How nice. Well, let's go back to our seat."

It was disconcerting to discover, in the lounge, that Mrs. Charlesworth had come noisily to life. Sister Wendy ran on ahead of the Joneses, to help Nurse Jackie. The Anthonys were still out.

"She's so strong, Sister," panted Nurse Jackie.

Mrs. Charlesworth was threatening Mr. Thomas with assault because he had paused in front of her.

"You stupid fool!" shrieked Mrs. Charlesworth, then shuddered into immobility.

"Thank heaven for that!" Sister Wendy took Mr. Thomas by the arm. "Come and sit down, precious, and have a read of your paper till tea-time."

"Tea-time?" Mr. Thomas brightened, glowed with relief. He looked up at the clock.

"Tea-time?" Mr. Weston cleared his throat. He was sitting in Miss Duncan's chair and Miss Duncan wasn't in the room. Helen, sinking into her own chair with Julian's assistance, found herself making a note of these things before remembering this was no longer necessary.

"Ah!" Sister Wendy was looking towards the door. "Here comes Mrs. Anthony."

The ponderous walk, which Helen was so much more used to hearing than seeing. The creak of the chair.

"I shan't linger, Mother, and anyway it's your tea-time soon." Miss Anthony was standing in front of the old lady, shifting from foot to foot.

"Good afternoon," said Julian.

"Good afternoon," muttered Miss Anthony. The wound was turning into a scar.

"Good afternoon!" said Mrs. Anthony brightly. "Hello, dear." A cool hand patted Helen's where they lay in her lap.

"Hello . . . I went out . . ."

"I'll be off now, Mother." Miss Anthony leaned forward to kiss the proffered cheek. Her hair, as usual, swung lank around her face. The mark on her cheek, today, was smaller and brighter.

"Will you come tomorrow, Mary?"

"I'll come tomorrow."

"Goodbye, dear." Mrs. Anthony settled back in her chair with a sigh. Miss Anthony moved out of Helen's vision, and Helen swallowed her heart down and stared steadily past Mr. Weston's bird-like gaze. Julian had her hand in his. There were no nursing staff in the room. It was too quiet . . . As Miss Welch's sister struck up a cheerful farewell across the room, Julian gathered up Helen's fingers and squeezed them.

The room swam in front of her as she leaned the little way that was necessary, turned her head so that she felt the white hair against her cheek.

"Mrs. Anthony," she said softly, "Miss Jones has more buttons on than you know. The game's up."

She drew back into her chair, and Mrs. Anthony so close beside her continued to sit stock-still. Helen began to wonder whether she ought to repeat herself. And then, it seemed at exactly the same moment, there was a sudden sharp movement of the white head and Rupert was standing behind Mrs. Anthony's chair.

"Oh no you don't," said Rupert, and Mrs. Anthony shot forward, stumbling to the floor. Something small and bright flew in an arc from her mouth and landed in the pattern of the carpet.

Julian was bending down, retrieving it. He and Rupert were hauling Mrs. Anthony, silent and unresisting, up on to her feet, walking her to the door and out. Miss Welch's sister was still saying goodbye. Miss Protheroe was looking out of the window. Mrs. Stoddart had fallen asleep again.

"Is Mrs. Anthony going out for tea?" asked Mr. Thomas, leaning forward, smiling.

"Tea-time soon," murmured Miss Jones.

Remain quietly seated.

Had the two men simply gone on walking Mrs. Anthony out of the front door and down the steps and into the car and away?

There were still no nursing staff in the room. Had they gone in pursuit of Julian? Might they catch him?

The stab of new life was as sharp and sudden as a knife

thrust. She had thought she didn't care, and she cared so much it was a pain in her heart.

Julian and Rupert. Miss Jones's brother and her nephew. So, it was known, now, that Miss Jones was not what she seemed. Somebody would have seen Miss Jones's brother and her nephew taking away the significant inmate of the lounge, if only through a camera's eye. So someone would arrange for action to be taken.

Julian. If I'm to go, I would rather it was you despatched me.

Remain quietly seated.

Remain waiting until they came for her. Because they would undoubtedly come. She had been set up as bait. Or why had Julian told her she was to defend herself? *But they were on the right side.*

Julian. Anger, and anguish. But nothing, really beyond the intensity of the moment.

CHAPTER 15

1

It was time for the clatter of crockery the far side of the dining-room door, but she couldn't hear anything. There were still no nursing staff in the room. Were they in conclave? Were they planning the form of their assault on the only remaining link with the hi-jacking of their agent?

Remain quietly seated. She didn't think she could turn her head, but the movement of her eyes showed her that the loud clock was reaching a quarter to four; that Mr. Thomas appeared to be asleep over his paper; that Miss Protheroe still regarded the cloud-strewn skies, Miss Welch continued to rake

Miss Jones with haunted anguish from across the room. She felt draught to either side of her, Mrs. Charlesworth sat so still. The clock crescendoed.

Remain quietly seated. But when there were all at once voices at the door, Helen made a little moaning sound.

"Miss Jones, dear, are you all right?" Nurse Jackie had perhaps heard her, if she hadn't been on her way over anyhow. "How about coming to the cloakroom with me, lovey, before tea?"

"Mary had a little lamb."

"There you are, yes, you're missing Mrs. Anthony. But it's all right, lovey, she went out with your brother and your nephew. Tracy told me, she was in the hall and saw them. I don't quite know why . . . and they didn't say when she was coming back, but of course it's all right . . . Not to worry, lovey, you come along with me."

And once in the cloakroom, never out of it again . . . Nurse Jackie. Somehow she had never thought . . . But Julian had always said, no preconceived ideas . . . *Not Julian.* Not so much because it hurt, she didn't have enough of herself available really to be hurt, but because it made her feel so fearfully muddled. She would like to have understood before . . .

"Don't want . . . want tea . . . Tea-time . . ."

"Is it tea-time?"

Mr. Thomas was craning round at the clock. Mrs. Stoddart was trying to get to her feet. As she had hoped, she had set the whole mechanical ballet in motion, spinning out the minutes . . .

"Nearly tea-time," said Nurse Jackie cheerfully. "And Mrs. Stoddart's coming to the cloakroom, aren't you, lovey?"

Nurse Jackie had Mrs. Stoddart by the arm. Miss Jones wavered to her feet.

"Cloakroom. I think I might . . ."

"That's right, precious. Come along."

Nurse Jackie let Miss Jones drift behind her and Mrs. Stoddart. It seemed a long, long walk across the lounge, the hall, into the cloakroom, the cubicle next to the cubicle where Nurse Jackie was half helping Mrs. Stoddart . . .

Miss Jones was fiddling with the towel on the back of the main door when Nurse Jackie moved away from the other cubicle and Mrs. Stoddart emerged.

"But we haven't washed our hands yet, have we, lovey?" Miss Jones and Mrs. Stoddart side by side at the washbasins, keeping identical pace. Both through the door and back into the hall together, like a small team being gently driven by Nurse Jackie. The dining-room doors open, now, into the lounge, the crockery sounds. Nurse Jackie steering her two charges straight through to their seats at table.

Tea-time . . . Helen found herself watching the origins of the dishes which were placed in front of her. It appeared that Nurse Jackie was picking up platefuls of macaroni cheese as it was ladled out and placed them round the tables in the normal logical order . . . And her tea came out of the pot just before Miss Protheroe's and just after Miss Duncan's . . .

Miss Duncan who hadn't appeared all afternoon in the lounge and had come last into the dining-room, looking ill in an unfamiliar way, heavy-eyed and unaccustomedly languid in her movements. It was several moments before she asked Miss Protheroe what had become of Mrs. Anthony.

"Mrs. Anthony went out," explained Miss Protheroe. "With Miss Jones's brother and nephew, actually, which struck me as a little . . . But her daughter had only just left, and so I suppose they had some arrangement . . ." Miss Protheroe smiled at Miss Jones, as if apologizing for the fact that she had had to speak for her, Miss Protheroe who had appeared to be watching her lap all the time Julian and Rupert had been in the lounge . . .

"I don't know what came over me this afternoon," said Miss Duncan. "But I felt so ill after lunch I had to lie down. And I fell asleep." Looking more herself by the minute, she fretfully clicked her tongue.

"I'm so sorry, dear," said Miss Protheroe, "and I must say that when you came in I thought you looked rather poorly. But you look better now."

"Not because of my tea."

The words were a sharp memory of Mrs. Wellington, and

Helen looked from one empty space to the other. Soon there would be a third . . . One thing at least she could control, her imagination.

She would have liked to go and sit in the kitchen after tea, however illogical the sense of safety it gave her, but she must go, as straight as Miss Jones ever went anywhere, to her chair in the lounge, and stay there. An entertaining film was the best thing she could hope for, and an old one was just coming up. Elegant, wise-cracking Americans in scratched black-and-white yet sumptuous Hollywood. It seemed amazing how, in what might be her final hours, she could enter for moments at a time those expensive rooms, take part in those witty gatherings . . .

"You really look as if you're enjoying yourself, Miss Jones, dear."

She welcomed the small test, and the fact that she had controlled her start of alarm. Sister Wendy was in Mrs. Anthony's chair, perched in her usual way as if poised for imminent take-off, smiling at Miss Jones, her fair hair springing free of her cap.

"Big man . . ." said Miss Jones, pointing vaguely towards a treble-chinned comedian.

"Yes, big man. Bedtime drink coming soon, lovey."

A hand momentarily on her shoulder, and Sister Wendy was swinging off across the room. Why were they bothering to keep up the farce? Julian had said years of weeks ago that some of them were no more than what they seemed, but others . . .

Well, Miss Jones was already out of character, sitting tight in the lounge for the whole of an evening, prepared to defend herself. Until she went up to bed . . . *Don't go to sleep.* Julian, my love, my own . . . How extraordinary, to be *angry*, that there might not be another chance to sleep beside Julian . . .

"Here we are, sweetheart."

Tracy with the bedtime drinks, the only time Tracy came into the lounge. Untidy and shuffle-footed as ever, going round the room with the trolley, saying good night and God bless in the doorway . . .

The News. A better economic prospect, a bus over a cliff in India, a footballer transferred for an enormous fee. There was perhaps a foolish comfort in being reminded the world existed, even if she wouldn't be part of it for much longer . . . But Julian had said something else. *There will be protection.* She must not contribute to her own end by pessimism, she must have faith—glorious, ridiculous faith in Julian, in God . . . Faith, after all, could move mountains . . .

The wave of hope, although it died, sustained her until Nurse Sandra was there, suggesting it was bedtime.

There was a hold-up leaving the lounge, because of Mr. Thomas getting up just before Miss Jones did, and pausing to comment on the everyday fact of Miss Duncan with a book. Eventually Nurse Sandra edged herself and Miss Jones past him. In the hall the hope briefly and absurdly revived with the sight and sound of Mrs. Wayne-Jenkins vigorously descending the stairs. The aggressive sanity seemed to reflect outwards . . .

Mrs. Wayne-Jenkins was wearing a skirt of large, loud checks which didn't quite tally at the side seams. She began to speak as soon as she saw Nurse Sandra.

"Nurse! The bulb has gone again in the desk lamp. It was only replaced last week, extremely tiresome. Will you please get me another one."

"In a moment, Mrs. Wayne-Jenkins, of course, when I've seen to Miss Jones."

"Nurse. I am not asking you to fit the bulb for me, I am merely asking you to unlock that secret cupboard of yours which contains it, and give it to me to insert. I hope I am not unreasonable."

Self-satisfaction pulsed against Mrs. Wayne-Jenkins's large outline, which had reached the hall.

"Of course not, Mrs. Wayne-Jenkins. I'll find you the bulb the very moment I've got Miss Jones upstairs and seen to her."

There seemed no end to the sinister ambiguities. But she had suppressed her shudder.

"It will take you perhaps sixty seconds, Nurse. Which will be neither here nor there to Miss Jones."

Oh, but it was a lifetime to the one who was drowning.

Helen felt the stiffening of Nurse Sandra's arm. "We'll follow you up, Mrs. Wayne-Jenkins."

Mrs. Wayne-Jenkins stared a moment, recognized defeat, and began to stump back up the stairs. She was standing by the cupboard when Nurse Sandra and Miss Jones reached the landing. And that protection Julian had promised?

"You all right now, Miss Jones, dear?"

"All right, yes. Nice girl . . ."

"I'll look in again a bit later, then. You get into bed now."

Nurse Sandra shut the bedroom door on Helen. Mrs. Wayne-Jenkins's voice booming in monologue from the landing was preferable to the silence which followed it.

Helen Markham had the idea of stooping down and looking under the beds, but it seemed that she was more securely locked inside Miss Jones than she had ever been, and Miss Jones would never do such a thing. She undressed and washed in her usual way and at her usual pace, got into bed, and lay down.

The sun had not long set and the sky was a soft clear pink, all clouds gone except for a pink-edged bank lying along the horizon . . . Was everything in the room just as it always was, the silence as total?

"There's a good girl!"

At least she could jerk under the bedclothes. Only she hadn't done, she had held her shock inside Miss Jones's prone body, slowly turning her head on the pillow as Nurse Sandra crossed to the window and closed the curtains. Then crossed the room again without pausing, said "Good night, Miss Jones" at the door, and shut it.

2

Anything which happened now would be sinister, because nothing more should happen until morning. *Don't go to sleep.*

She didn't know the geographical lay-out of the United States, but she might manage them alphabetically. *Count on your fingers . . .*

Alaska, Alabama, Arizona . . .

She was almost falling asleep and then jerking awake. *Arkansas . . .* Almost drifting into the normal nightly state of relaxation and forgetfulness and then realizing, against all the instincts of her tired body, that she was in mortal danger.

California, Delaware, Florida . . .

It must have been like that in the condemned cell—the extraordinary, unbelievable paradox of knowing you were well and strong, and knowing you were about to die . . . Odious pessimism, she was not going to die. *There will be protection.*

Iowa, Indiana, Illinois . . . and another somewhere. Little Dolly Daydream, the pride of Idaho . . .

Where had that come from? She had no idea. What else lay at the dark base of one's mind, awaiting a context?

Kansas, Kentucky . . .

Sodium yellow shone steadily now through the curtains. The night was an eternity. If she lasted it out.

Montana, Maryland, Maine . . .

She had cramp in a finger, she was actually concentrating one hundred per cent, for moments at a time, on remembering these names . . . Her mind, herself, Helen Markham, couldn't go into oblivion, cease to exist, whatever happened to her body . . .

Michigan, Missouri, Mississippi . . .

Was that the Swanee River? Was there a creaking sound somewhere in the room? There was the thud of her heart in her ears, which she must strain above to listen to the quality of the silence.

Way down upon the Swanee River . . .

If only she was the disembodied mind she felt herself, immune to the pains that could be inflicted on her body. She hadn't revolted against the idea of Julian killing her. But this was different . . .

Nebraska, Nevada, North Carolina . . .

She was leaning over, clutching the cold edge of the bed,

trying to control the trembling of her fear. Fear which would
make her sick if it persisted, only it couldn't persist like that,
nothing could . . .

Lie quiet, don't think of anything. Just say those words
again. And again. *There will be protection. There will be protection. There will be protection.*

But don't go to sleep.

Oregon, Oklahoma, Ohio . . .

And a sound at the door, the door very gently opening, she
could see its white edge advancing by the grey light of the
window, for the moment an absurd sense of relief . . . Then
nothing at all beyond just being, just getting from moment to
moment . . .

The figure in nurse's uniform was silently shutting the door.
Gliding towards the bed. Sitting down on it and leaning forward with a hand to either side of Miss Jones. Switching on
the little spot light above the bed. Smiling. Only the big blue
eyes were cold.

"Hello, Miss Jones, precious."

"Nice girl . . ." It seemed that there really was a Miss Jones.
It couldn't be that Helen Markham had had anything to do
with that thin vague voice, that inappropriate sentiment.

Sister Wendy laughed. The same laugh as always, but this
time infinitely unamused. As was the brilliance of the blue
eyes, the width of the smile on the beautiful mouth.

"You're a very good actress, lovey," said Sister Wendy gaily.
"You deceived me, and you have deceived Mary, even when
she hurt you. That I have to admire. Even while I'm angry.
And I'm very, very angry."

Sister Wendy brought her lovely face down to the face looking blankly up at her from the bed. The face which had locked
itself as never before into the incomprehension of Miss Jones,
wouldn't unlock, wouldn't give the satisfaction . . . *Best not to
fight your own battle.*

"Hickorydickorydock!"

The movement was so quick she seemed to see Sister
Wendy's hand drop to her side the same moment she felt the
stinging split at the corner of her mouth. She heard Miss Jones

whimpering, helping Helen Markham to stay hidden. There was wet warmth on her chin.

"Oh, clever." Sister Wendy's voice was more sibilant now, a soft hiss. How could it ever have seemed that her mouth was beautiful? "But too clever, I think, too clever by half, because if I wasn't so angry I might make it quicker . . . Speak to me, damn you."

The second blow was far, far more painful. After it even Miss Jones couldn't say anything, but she still looked blankly at Sister Wendy, uncomprehending . . .

"You bloody bitch. I wanted to make you . . . I wanted you to tell me . . . But I don't want you to tell anyone else, so I can't hang about. A pity, I'm enjoying myself."

As the young man had enjoyed himself in the corridor in the night. The blood now was visible, crawling across the sheet. *Best not to fight your own battle. There will be protection.*

"Two up and one to go. Mary and her mother had one each. Well, Mary had two, but I think she was a wee bit over-zealous. And now it's my turn. At least I can complete the set before I disappear. I have to disappear now, Miss Jones, because of you. You've spoiled my set-up, but I can spoil your future. Well, I don't exactly mean spoil, I mean make sure you don't have any. I've got a gun if you try to resist me, but I think we'll do what we did before. And really, how could anyone regret the fact of poor Miss Jones dying in her sleep?"

There was a ghastly gurgle of laughter, and Sister Wendy had a syringe in her hand. Helen, half-anaesthetized by the impregnable coating of Miss Jones, felt she had seen it already, a long time ago . . . "Little lamb. Little lamb . . ." The syringe was coming towards her, any second now she would feel . . .

But the syringe was still in mid-air and with a soft plop it was exploding . . . No, not exploding, falling intact into the eiderdown where it poised quivering, and there were dark patches falling on the sheet. Not from the syringe but from Sister Wendy's wrist, that was what had exploded, and Sister Wendy was holding it in her other hand as she rocked and moaned. There was a young man beside her, hitting her

on the neck so that she fell off the bed on to the floor. No, not
a young man, Tracy in shirt and jeans, a gun in her hand, already at the window. No, not a gun, a torch . . .

A voice was screaming somewhere . . . Was it Miss Jones,
or Helen Markham? Screaming on and on. Tracy was back by
the bed. It wasn't a torch in her hand, it was another syringe.
She couldn't escape this one, she had done all she could, and
Sister Wendy would never meet Helen Markham. Never.
Never . . . Julian . . . I don't understand, but I would just like
to have seen you once again.

3

When she woke up, or the dream changed, Julian seemed to
be sitting by the bed, and in the stillness and silence there
were recent vague memories of movement and voices. Julian
was casually dressed and young-looking with untidy hair—the
way she most liked him to look, and of course in dreams you
could sometimes choose. He was relaxed, smiling at her. She
smiled back on a reflex, before frowning. Partly because it hurt
her to smile, and also because she remembered fear and danger and deceit and his association with them. Julian said
softly, "No need to worry, darling. Any more."

He was stroking her forehead, his hand cool and dry.

"I don't understand." She was crying, discovering how weak
she felt, how sore her mouth was. "Julian, Sister Wendy . . .
And suddenly Tracy . . ."

"Tracy was in the empty wardrobe, the one Mrs. Barker had.
She was there when you came upstairs, waiting for you, then
waiting with you. You've slept peacefully for hours and hours.
Through a day and a night. Sister Wendy split your lip and
bruised your cheek. How do you feel otherwise?"

"I feel all right. But I shan't be all right until I know what's
been happening. And what's going to happen. Julian. Please."

"Of course." There was a knock at the door. "Come in." It
was Tracy again, carrying a tray and wearing her kitchen
clothes. "Here's some breakfast."

"I don't want any breakfast. I only want to know what all this is about. That's all I want, and I really want it." She heard herself petulant, and saw Tracy glance at Julian.

"Of course you do, and as soon as you've eaten and drunk something you'll get what you really want. But you must have some nourishment. It's only boiled egg and toast and tea. You can have it at Helen Markham's pace and it'll take ten minutes. Then if you feel up to it put on your dressing-gown and come to Matron's room."

"Miss Jones?"

"Poor Miss Jones. She fell the night before last and cut her face. The doctor came and sedated her for shock. Her brother's taking her back with him this morning."

Tracy had gone and he bent to kiss her on the healthy side of her mouth. She didn't respond.

"Miss Jones doesn't wear a dressing-gown."

"We'll risk it," he said, and left her.

At once she began to eat, she did feel all right, if a bit headachy and with a throbbing pulse at the corner of her mouth so that she must eat carefully. And sick for a moment, as she moved the tray to look at the sheet. But it was clean, and she finished what Tracy had brought her.

All that mattered, now, was her ignorance. She put the tray aside and got out of bed, made it across the room with only a slight sensation of giddiness. She washed her face, cleaned her teeth, and combed her hair, feeling her strength return. She put on the new dressing-gown Miss Jones had not yet worn, then went along to the bathroom, locking the door behind her. The shiny distortion spreading from her mouth made her look like someone she had never seen before, but perhaps the encounter was easier for that. When she came out of the bathroom she drifted down the corridor and, making sure she was unobserved, knocked at Matron's door.

4

Standing, it seemed casually, round Matron's desk were Julian, Mrs. Roberts, Matron and Tracy. She could only have been

more astonished if Sister Wendy had been there too, more
dizzy and confused. Julian came forward and caught her as
she stumbled towards them, helped her into one of the chairs
beside the desk.

"I'm sorry," she murmured, her forehead on the desk edge.

"No need to be, Mrs. Markham."

She was able to sit upright and see that it was Mrs. Roberts
speaking, smiling.

"Please . . ."

"Mr. Jones," said Mrs. Roberts good-humouredly, "you really must tell her the truth."

"I know." Julian pulled a chair out beside Helen and sat
down, taking her hand. Everyone else sat down somewhere
round the desk. Through the half-open window she could hear
the insistent voice of a thrush, and the sun was slanting across
Mrs. Roberts's pale hair. "Helen. We in this room, we're all On
Her Majesty's Service."

"That's right, dear," supplemented Mrs. Roberts. Whatever
Helen had expected at this moment it was never, in her suc-
cessive nightmares, an amicable conversation. But with relief
came fury. She pulled her hand away.

"Oh, thank you. What fun you must have had!"

"Helen . . ."

"Mrs. Markham," said Matron, "please listen. We realize
there are a great many things to explain." The voice was
different, soft and low. And the face, in a way Helen couldn't
define. And only Tracy, of all those at the desk, looked anything like strong and invulnerable.

"I should think there are!" The fury was warming, enliven-
ing.

"I told you," said Julian, not attempting to repossess himself
of her hand, "that Hill House was a temporary refuge for
enemy agents. What I did not tell you is that the agents, and
hence those on the staff who are briefed to their presence, are
British."

"God, Julian—"

"Hill House is what is known as a safe house. Agents need
places in their own countries to cope with illnesses and conva-

lescences and the need to disappear temporarily when heat is on and they daren't be seen in their usual haunts. We needed you because we knew there was a KGB agent among the Hill House patients, operating in conjunction with another KGB agent on the staff—which meant almost certainly Matron, Mrs. Roberts or Sister Wendy, the three members of staff ostensibly working with the British Service. If you'd known all the staff but one were either ignorant that it was a safe house or on your side, you would surely, at some point, have relaxed your vigilance, come out of your role, for a second which would have been observed by that one person. The only way to keep you safe was to make you afraid of everyone, all the time. And the only way to do that was to stand the truth on its head." He had her hand again, was pressing it. "Helen, God knows I've wanted to put you straight, I've been tempted . . . But so long as you weren't sure you could relax in any situation, you were comparatively safe."

"And comparatively useful."

"That, too," he said evenly. "And it had to work the other way as well. None of our staff knew you were more than Miss Jones or I more than her brother, because all of them were under suspicion. Except for Tracy, who was brought in to keep some kind of an eye on you. Even when Rupert and I took Mrs. Anthony away and Tracy made sure everyone was aware of how she had left, only one person knew the significance of it."

"Wendy," murmured Matron. "Even now I can't . . ." Her voice was husky, and there was a tear on her lashes. With a brief effort of the imagination Helen saw the two women relaxing after weeks of mutual mistrust, while knowing for certain the treachery of the third. It must be a horrible sensation. Her sensations were horrible, too.

"You set me up." She was pleased to hear how flat and indifferent her voice was.

Julian said firmly, "Yes. We knew after we took Mrs. Anthony away that our mole might try to dispose of you before disappearing."

"Tracy might have acted sooner," said Helen pettishly.

"I wanted to hear all there was to be heard." The kindest one now seemed the coolest. "But I wasn't going to let anything happen to you."

"I may not have had a hypodermic in my arm," said Helen, "well, not a lethal one, but how can you possibly know that nothing's happened to me?"

It was as if she wanted something luxurious for a change, and anger would do.

"We can't," murmured Julian, his eyes on the desk.

"We know how you must feel, Mrs. Markham." The gentle voice was the matron's. It might be interesting to ponder how as an actress, the suppression of natural warmth had altered this woman, without any modification to her physical appearance . . . Impatiently she spurned her drifting thoughts, marshalling her anger, angry that their reasonableness threatened it. She stood up.

"I'd like to get dressed."

"Of course." Everyone else stood up too.

"Miss Jones," said Julian apologetically. "I'll come along in a few moments."

"Congratulations again," said Mrs. Roberts, and there was a supportive murmur. It was satisfying to ignore it, and silently leave the room.

Back in her bedroom she was Helen Markham, moving swiftly about, impelled by the energy of her anger. But small bubbles of understanding, despite herself, kept breaking surface.

Julian had been anxious for her safety.

For her usefulness. She had been grotesquely deceived. She flung about, not wasting a moment in which she might be free of them.

But the bubbles were getting bigger. Julian preferred her to distrust him than to add to her peril.

And detract from her usefulness. They had so completely deceived her, and she had questioned nothing, only the one thing which was the truth. She strode up and down, glimpsing the possibility that her anger was really against herself.

"Ready, sweetheart?"

Julian was in the doorway, and she had more perverse satisfaction in sitting in the armchair while he packed Miss Jones's bag. He left some things in wardrobe and drawers.

"All set then, I think."

Silently they crossed the landing and descended the stairs. Passing the lounge she remembered something else.

"Where was Miss Duncan yesterday afternoon?" It was a muted protest, because she scarcely moved her lips.

He answered as softly, "Sleeping off a rather particular glass of barley water. She's too clever by half."

"And what are you?"

And what am I?

Julian rang the bell, and Nurse Jackie was instantly with them.

"Good morning, Mr. Jones. I hear you're taking your sister . . ." Nurse Jackie broke off as she saw Helen's face, began to look embarrassed at her open reaction, then realized that with Miss Jones it didn't matter. "Poor love!" Nurse Jackie squeezed her shoulder. "You let your brother bring you back to us as soon as possible!"

"Nice girl . . ."

Nurse Jackie was a nice girl. And Miss Protheroe a nice little woman. And the air warm and soft on her face.

"There we are, then!"

She had forced him to use a little strength, to get her into the front seat of the car. As they drove between the posts she whispered fiercely, "I want to walk by the sea. Now. There's miles of shore, you can find a spot."

"All right." He sounded unconcerned.

"Thank you." She didn't say it until he drew up on a stretch of road immediately above the beach. She opened the car door, got out, and began to stride off as if she was alone, her senses tingling. Scent of pines and petrol. Breeze, sun on her neck. Holiday voices. Spring. She was entering the steep cut to the shore down which so many careless people went.

"Hold on a bit." Julian put a hand on her arm and she slowed grudgingly to a stroll. "That's better. When are you going to run out of steam?"

"It's all very well for you to be amused."

"I'm not amused."

She didn't answer, but despite herself she was responding favourably to the delicious assault of her freedom, the sounds, the sights, the space, the end of vigilance. At the foot of the descent she sat down on a low wall and pulled off the tights she had just put on, stuffing them into Miss Jones's shoes. The road was rough to her feet, and then she was in the sand, kneading it with her toes.

Julian had accepted her lead, but now he said, "Away from the town, I think," and silently she turned beside him and they began to walk parallel with the water. She was doing one of the things she had longed for, and she could do it again, and again.

If Julian wanted to do it, too.

She wasn't angry, she was desperately anxious. When their hands brushed against each other he made no effort to catch her fingers. Her restored freedom could be the richest thing in the world, or the most desolate.

"Sit down?" he asked, when there was a desert of yellow-gold space around them. The question broke their long silence.

"Why not."

She hugged her knees, nestling herself a seat in the sand, admitting her self-dissatisfaction. If she hadn't been so dignified, she would probably know by now whether or not he loved her.

"You'd like me to fill in the gaps."

"Of course." She hadn't given them a thought. She made an effort. "What happens now at Hill House?"

"Hill House quietly becomes nothing more than a nursing home. Well, of course it is really only that already. Once we knew it had been infiltrated. Mrs. Roberts and Matron, having two careers, will leave and disappear, the others I suppose will continue."

"What about Mr. Weston?" She was keeping it going automatically, but she supposed that, somewhere, she wanted to know.

"He's not involved in our business, but we'll tip off the local station—his behaviour in the vicinity of policemen does rather suggest there's a little more to it than picking up Miss Jones's powder compact. Probably only petty theft, but maybe also from one or two of the hotels where he has his regular whiskies."

"Mr. Weston drinks in hotels?" It was absurd, that this small revelation should have more impact on her than the larger ones. "Did Miss Anthony kill Mrs. Wellington?"

"Not a doubt of it."

"But she wasn't—one of you?"

"Oh no. And she could hardly have known anything she shouldn't have known. She was just rather perceptive. And I suppose she might have made some further unwelcome pronouncements."

"Julian . . ." *Mary and her mother had one each.* If she was going to be angry, she should be angry over this. But she wasn't angry over anything at all. "I know why you really wanted me. I know two people had been killed. One by each of the Anthonys."

He had turned to look at her in his old, intensified way.

"Yes. Two of our best agents. I don't think I was going to tell you. I suppose Sister Wendy . . ."

"Just about."

"Helen . . ."

"No, it's all right. You were doing your job."

"Thank you."

"Is Cora really your daughter?"

This time they turned towards one another on an instant. She swallowed her heart down, sifting sand through her fingers.

"Does it matter?" he asked. "Are you anxious to know?" He was gazing at her searchingly and she had to look down at her busy hand.

"Not really. Perhaps it's more—interesting—not to know."

Or less agonizing. Children. A mother . . .

"But I shall tell you. I have a daughter. Not Cora. A nephew. Not Rupert. And . . ."

"Yes?" She took her hand out of the sand, held it against her heart.

"I have no wife."

"And listen carefully now, because I won't say this often, if ever again. I love you madly."

She still didn't look up.

"You, Julian Jones?"

"I, whoever I am."

"Whoever I am, I love you too."

On an instant, again, they looked at one another. On an instant they felt for each other's hand. It was the best moment of her life, whoever she was. Suddenly she could hardly talk enough.

"Julian, I've just realized . . . all this acting . . . and thinking about identity, panicky sometimes that mine was slipping away. I've just realized . . . I've never been so much me before, in my whole life. And the real play-acting . . . Julian, how can you live for years and not even know you're playing a part?"

"Mrs. John Markham?"

"The most preposterous farce of all. When I was so sure I knew just what was what."

"Have you always played a part?"

She considered, holding his hand against her cheek. "Not as a child. I lost it all—or buried it all—so gradually I couldn't say when . . . I suppose I was more me when I was Miss Jones, really, because I knew for certain that so much of what I was doing wasn't me. Does that sound too ridiculous?"

"No. In losing yourself, you found yourself again."

"Perhaps. Anyway, I found *you*. You-and-me, that's real enough."

"Do you want to go on working?"

"I'm not so sure about that."

"I am. I know you. I've seen you. Your stamina, Mrs. Barker. When you were ill. You can't have that sort of strength and not want to use it for what you believe in. The only time I lost you was in those last hours at The Laurels."

"I lost myself then. I didn't want to do anything except sit

in a chair and read. Because I couldn't let myself think . . .
You're right, I suppose, I shall want to go on working. I see
now, by the way, why you were so interested in the young
man—he was the only character in my reports you didn't know
about already."

"I confess it. Whose pocket did you find those papers in?"

"I really am not going to tell you. Which I realize is to tell
you that it wasn't Sister Wendy's. Julian, when you asked me
that question about Tracy, about whether she was professional
when she went for the young man—were you afraid she might
have given herself away?"

"Yes."

"She didn't. She was clever."

"So were you. Also long-suffering and of great goodness."

"I can't believe this is me being so happy."

He brought an envelope out of his pocket.

"At least there is no one else for whom this is intended."

The envelope was addressed to her in John's writing. It had
been opened.

"Regulations again," he said ruefully.

"So you've read it."

"Duty and inclination for once coinciding."

There were two sheets, on which John told her he had made
a mistake and wanted her to go back to him. She looked at the
date.

"Strictly," she said, "you should have given me this earlier.
Were you uncertain of me?"

"I told you once," he said, "that I only had hope."

"I'm glad you waited."

Slowly she tore the letter in half, into four pieces, then
eight. As she had torn John's photograph at Mrs. Molyneux's,
the beginning of her recovery, and the end. She put the pieces
back into the envelope and gave it to him.

"I don't approve of litter," she said, "but in this case . . ."

Solemnly they dug a hole, as deep as fingernails could make
it, and buried the envelope. They looked about them, and the
nearest figure was still a dot. They put their arms round one
another.

M48

They brushed the sand off each other's clothes.
"Julian, I want to turn cartwheels. I must be mad."
"Whoever you are."
"Whoever I am."
Hand in hand they started to make their way back along the shore.

Eileen Dewhurst was born in Liverpool and educated there at Huyton College, and later at Oxford. As a free-lance journalist, she has published many articles in the *Liverpool Daily Post*, the *Illustrated Liverpool News*, *Punch*, and *The Times*. She has written plays that have been performed in England, and is the author of five previous crime novels, including *Curtain Fall*, *Trio in Three Flats*, and *Drink This*.